P9-CEM-592

Read This and Tell Me What It Says

A. Manette Ansay

Read This and Tell Me What It Says

F
Ansa

University of Massachusetts Press · Amherst

8/96   *Brodart*   *22.95*

This book is the winner of the Associated Writing Programs 1994 Award in Short Fiction. AWP is a national, nonprofit organization dedicated to serving American letters, writers, and programs of writing. AWP's headquarters are at George Mason University, Fairfax, Virginia.

Library of Congress Cataloging-in-Publication Data
Ansay, A. Manette.
Read this and tell me what it says / A. Manette Ansay.
p.   cm.
ISBN 0–87023–988–0
1. Wisconsin—Social life and customs—Fiction.
2. City and town life—Wisconsin—Fiction.
3. Community life—Wisconsin—Fiction.
4. Country life—Wisconsin—Fiction.   I. Title.
PS3551.N645R43   1995
813'.54—dc20   95–11039
CIP

British Library Cataloguing in Publication data are available.

this book is dedicated to my computer consultant
Jake Smith

Though I know my complaint is bitter, his hand is heavy upon me . . .

BOOK OF JOB, CHAPTER 23

Acknowledgments

The author gratefully acknowledges the magazines that first published these stories, some in slightly different form:

Black Warrior Review 21, no. 1 (Fall/Winter 1994): "Spot Weakness";

Chicago Tribune, September 27, 1992, © 1992 Chicago Tribune Company. All rights reserved; used with permission: "Read This and Tell Me What It Says";

Columbia: A Magazine of Poetry and Prose: "Smoke";

The Crescent Review, Fall 1994: "You or Me or Anything" and "Evolution of Dreams";

EPOCH 44, no. 3: "Neighbor";

The Greensboro Review 58 (Summer 1995): "Lost Objects";

The North American Review: "Silk" and "Sybil";

Northwest Review 29, no. 2 (1991): "The Trial";

Quarterly West 32 (Winter/Spring 1991): "Infidel";

The Southern Review 30, no. 2, n.s. (Spring 1994): "Ohio";

13th Moon: "Lies"

"Lessons" has been anthologized in *Word of Mouth*, vol 2: *Short Short Stories by Women*, ed. Irene Zahava (The Crossing Press, 1991). "Sybil" has been anthologized in *The Pushcart Prize* 19: *Best of the Small Presses.* "July" has been anthologized in *American Fiction* (New Rivers Press, 1995).

The author (again) thanks the MFA program at Cornell University for financial support during an early draft of this collection. Special thanks to the faculty, especially my committee, James McConkey and Maureen McCoy, and to Kim Dionis, Stewart O'Nan, Kyna Taylor, and the rest of the 1989–1991 workshop.

Thanks to Phillips Exeter Academy, where the collection took its adult shape, and to Vanderbilt University, where the final stories were written.

Acknowledgments

The author expresses special gratitude to the *Chicago Tribune* which awarded "Read This and Tell Me What It Says" the Nelson Algren Prize in 1992. More thanks to *Columbia: A Magazine of Poetry and Prose* for awarding "Smoke" an Editor's Choice Prize and to *American Fiction* for awarding "July" second place in its annual fiction contest.

Thanks to Elizabeth Tallent and the Associated Writing Programs for choosing this book for publication and to the University of Massachusetts Press for making it a tangible thing. And finally, I thank my tireless and resourceful marketing specialist, Dick Ansay, my insightful editor, Sylvia J. Ansay, and my cousin David O. Krier for his encouragement.

Contents

Read This and Tell Me What It Says

Lost Objects

At night, my brother heard wolves in the corn. There were no wolves left in southeastern Wisconsin, but Alex had seen their yellow-slit eyes, their long teeth brighter than moonlight. He listened to them mutter in the language of wolves on those nights when he crouched by my window, shivering in his BVD's, staring out at the cornfield that began ten feet from the house. Occasionally, we'd see the glowing eyes of a deer or raccoon or one of the tiger-striped cats that lived, half wild, in the barn. Once we saw a fox, brief as a breath of smoke. But the wolves stayed slyly hidden, slipping between the stalks only when the wind blew, rustling the leaves with their tails.

"Wolves," Alex told me, "are smarter than most people. They are smarter than astronauts and doctors. They live in cities built deep under the ground."

We were sitting in the apple tree we'd claimed for our own by carving our initials near the top. It was June, and most of the tree was still in blossom; if I squinted, the petals blurred and made the leaves look like they were covered in snow. But Alex didn't seem to notice the blossoms, or the bees hanging above our heads, or the sound the bees made which rose and fell like the sound of someone breathing.

"The mind of a wolf is like a maze," he said. "No human being can figure out exactly how it works."

"What about scientists?" I said.

"When the moon is full," Alex said, ignoring me, "wolves speak in a language no one else can understand."

His pale hair reached to his shoulder blades; the soles of his feet, dangling near my head, were stained the color of grass. I listened to him as politely as I could, but I preferred my own thoughts to my brother's, and I wanted to go back to the house and lie on my bed, as I often did for hours, letting the breeze from the open windows ruffle over me. My bedroom had once been my mother's, and it still had the same pink walls and gray trim, the lacy white curtains, the bed frame carved with flowers that my grandfather had finished just one day before he died. Alex's room faced the highway where he claimed the wolves were afraid to go; he bribed me with candy and cap pistols and robin's eggs, but I wouldn't trade rooms because I loved to lie in bed and imagine my mother as a young girl. She'd been bright, I knew, and pretty. She liked to read, and filled sketchbooks with drawings of flowers and sunsets and trees. At night, I fell asleep imagining the sound of her voice, and in the morning, when I woke up, I could hear her talking quietly to my grandmother in their room. Sometimes Alex would still be under my window, wrapped in the bear's paw quilt he'd swiped from the foot of my bed, his pale hair glowing sunlight. After breakfast, after chores, we walked down to the orchard and climbed into our tree, looking out across the fruit trees and the surrounding fields of corn, past the house and the barn and the milkhouse forming a crescent around the courtyard, down the dirt road which led to the highway, searching for the subtle signs a careless wolf might leave behind.

We had moved in with my grandmother at the beginning of the summer, after my father announced he was hitching west to California with a woman named Marge. He brought her to our house just before they left: my mother served coffee while Alex and I sat on the couch, dressed in Sunday clothes, snitching candy raisins from the glass bowl on the coffee table. Marge had wrinkly hair and a laugh that echoed in our ears like a slap. She called us *kiddos* and my mother *dear*. She and my father sat side by side on the padded folding chairs my mother brought out for company.

"I want all of you to get along," my father said. He kept his hand on Marge's arm as if he thought she might jump up at any moment.

He looked unfamiliar, and I stared at him until my mother tapped my knee with her finger, her signal that I shouldn't be rude. She wore a white dress printed with yellow and pink flowers; her hair was braided neatly and tied with a pink ribbon. She looked fresh and bright as a doll, with her pretty dress and tiny doll's feet, and watching her, I felt proud. But when she poured coffee into my father's cup, her hand shook, and coffee spilled down the front of her dress.

"Oh, I'm so sorry," she said to no one in particular.

"I always do things like that," Marge said, and she laughed her ringing laugh. She wore jeans and a man's flannel shirt, untucked. Her hair was cut short; practical hair. "If you use cold water right away it won't stain."

"I'm so embarrassed," my mother said. She did not leave to wash it out with cold water. Instead, she scrubbed at the brown streak with her napkin. By the time my father and Marge stood up to go, it had faded almost gold. My father kissed me, suddenly, on the forehead. The kiss sounded like stepping in something wet. I wiped it away and my father laughed.

"These kids are too old for kissing," he said. Then he shook Alex's hand. From the way Alex bit his lip I could tell my father had squeezed too hard.

"We'll be sure and write you kiddos soon," Marge said.

And, after we'd moved to my grandmother's, we did get one postcard in a strange, spiky hand: *Dear Alex and Susan, Today we saw mountains bigger than anything you can imagine. Love, your dad and Marge.*

"She means the Rocky Mountains," Alex said. "They aren't so much." He tore the postcard into many tiny pieces and threw those pieces away.

Nothing interested Alex as much as wolves. He kept a shoe box underneath his bed, and this shoe box was filled with photographs of wolves, articles about wolves, and plaster of Paris casts of what he said were wolf tracks. On hot days, we crept into the coolness of the

3

cornfield, looking for wolf scat and wolf kills and clumps of wolf hair fine as goose down. The cornfield was off-limits to us, not only because we could damage the stalks, but because my mother had heard of two children, an eleven-year-old and a ten-year-old, by chance the exact ages of Alex and me, who had wandered into a cornfield and walked for days, lost among the long green rows, the tassels waving high above their heads. When these children were found, of course, they were dead: my mother said from dehydration, but Alex knew better.

"Wolves," he whispered later into the darkness of my room. "They came while those children slept and sucked their blood through a tooth mark the size of a pin."

"What happens if the wolves suck *your* blood?" I asked, but Alex just shook his head. I was not afraid because, in my heart, I did not believe in the wolves, and Alex was not afraid because he believed in the wolves the way my grandmother believed in God, the way my mother believed my father's affair would pass like any season.

"Steve will be home in fall," she told my grandmother, my aunts, anyone who would listen. My mother was the sort of person who saw the glass half full, never half empty. She always was certain that something good was waiting for each of us right around the corner. She never learned to recognize sadness: ours, my father's, or her own.

"Wolves," Alex said, "are quieter than angels. They can suck away your blood before you know what they have done."

I was born with six fingers on each hand. The extras, which my mother refused to describe, were removed soon after I was born, leaving shiny oblong scars that stayed pale in summer when my hands turned brown. I could not forgive my mother for not having any photographs of those fingers. I could not forgive her for not knowing where, exactly, those fingers were now.

"Are they buried?" I asked her. "Can you tell me if they're buried?"

My mother was sitting on the screen porch, reading a paperback romance. Others were piled next to her, some with crisp bright covers, some held together with tape. Empty diet soda cans were stacked beside the books. I stood outside, speaking through the screen. When my father lived with us, my mother had always answered such questions by saying, *Go ask your Dad.* Now, she licked a finger, turned a page, slowly, deliberately.

"Do you want a soda pop?" she said. "Susan? Come have a soda."

I ran my fingernails over the screen; her shoulders twitched, then froze. "I'm not thirsty," I said. "Are they in a museum? When I die, do I get them back?"

She twisted to stare at me, marking her place in her book with her finger. I stared back without blinking, my chin out, my back straight. Soon my eyes began to water; finally, my mother looked away.

"Go ask your grandmother," she said.

I did not move. My grandmother considered the topic unwholesome: those fingers, like the rest of me, were God's will, so why worry about it? Whenever she heard me pestering my mother, she found some sort of work for me to do. *The shelves in the pantry need fresh paper,* she'd say, or, *There's thistles coming up in the beans.* So I ambushed my mother when I knew she'd be alone: on her way out to the barn, working in the garden, or, like now, reading on the porch.

"Will they rot?" I asked. "Are there just bones left? If they get attached to someone else, will they grow?"

"I don't know, I don't know," my mother said. Her hair, braided into one long tail, fell almost to her waist. She had a habit of taking the tip and rubbing it against the side of her neck when something made her unhappy. "Why does it matter so much?" she said. "Why do you *think* about such things?"

I couldn't *not* think about it. *Your body is God's temple,* I was told again and again, but a part of my temple had been cut away at birth, and for all I knew, part of my soul as well. I watched my mother drag the tip of her braid up and down the side of her neck. In a way, she looked younger than I did: she was gentle, dreamy, someone to be protected.

"You sure you don't want a soda?" she said. Her lips were white; she turned back to her book, stared into it fiercely. She turned a page, then another. The book trembled in her hand. I came in and opened a soda, which I ended up leaving untouched. I didn't ask any more questions.

But I began to have dreams about my fingers. I dreamed I saw them dangling like earrings from a stranger's pierced ears. I dreamed I was chewing a tough piece of meat: I spat, and out came my fingers. I'd wake up crying and squeeze into bed between the warm bodies of my mother and my grandmother, elbowing the dog to the floor, scattering the cats. *Sh, sh,* my grandmother said, stroking my back while my mother lay rigid, not knowing what to do. Eventually, after an exchange of whispers, one of them got the whiskey from the medicine chest and fed it to me by the tablespoon until I began to relax. The dog returned, put his cool nose to my forehead; the cats crouched on the dresser top, their eyes flashing occasional, vivid green. I fell asleep, lulled by the ticking of the old wind-up clock on the nightstand, my grandmother's hand in my hair.

In the basement, next to the root cellar door, was a damp wooden cabinet filled with old photographs: weddings, funerals, solemn children dressed in tattered gray clothes. I spent hours looking at those photographs, because one night my grandmother had told me, hoping to distract me from my crying, that her mother's sister had had six fingers just like me. Her name had been Gerta Bruch, but when we went downstairs together to look at the photographs, my grandmother could not remember which one she was.

"It must be the light," she said. Her voice was small; bewildered.

The only light was a bare bulb that hung from the ceiling at the foot of the stairs. The basement floor was made of packed dirt; the walls were covered by shelves filled with canning jars, broken tools, wire, bits of brick, baling twine. Shadows from the shelves wobbled over the floor; the light seemed to move, sliding behind the broken generator, the chipped freezer, the coil of cracked rubber tubing.

"I'll get the flashlight," I said, and I ran back up to the top of the stairs where my grandmother kept one hanging on a hook. But even direct light didn't help; my grandmother held the photographs first close to her face, then far away. She took off her glasses. She put them back on.

"I suppose it doesn't matter," she finally said. "They're dead, so it makes no difference now."

But it made a difference to me. I searched the faces again and again for something—I didn't know what—I was sure I would recognize. One day, when I'd been looking at the photographs for a long time, the eyes of my relatives began to follow mine, and I saw their lips part ever so slightly. *Tell me, tell me who she is,* I whispered, and they smiled slightly as if they knew what they had to say I could not understand. Gerta Bruch was never revealed to me, though I prayed to her, to all of them, on my knees: desperate, angry prayers.

My mother was the youngest child, shy and sweet, the family favorite. After my grandfather died, she moved into my grandmother's room and they slept like spoons every night until, at twenty, she left home to marry my father. My father moved her to Detroit, two hundred miles away, and for the first year of their marriage my mother would lie awake most of the night, unable to sleep without her mother's soft back, without the guilty noises her two older sisters made slipping softly into the house after curfew. Only after Alex was born was she able to sleep soundly, his head tucked under her chin, her body curved around his body, protecting him from my father's restless limbs.

Sometimes I'd spy on my mother and my grandmother, watching the way their heads nearly touched as they hulled berries at the kitchen table; the identical stiffness of their backs as they walked down the hill to the orchard. There was something between them, an invisible current, that made the movement of one seem connected to the movement of the other. It was a slow, gentle dance, their bodies anticipating each other, graceful, bending, giving way.

My aunts, who lived close by with their own families, teased my mother, calling her *mama's girl.* But they, too, treated her with special care, fussing over her, shaking their heads. "Oh, *Honey,*" they'd say when my mother forgot the sugar in the rhubarb pies, or left the truck lights on overnight. My grandmother, too, called her Honey; I had never heard anybody, even my father, address her by her real name, Joanne.

No one could believe it when my father left. *The bastard,* Aunt Libby hissed to Aunt Dora in the pantry; when they looked up and saw me listening, their faces turned dark as plums. I went back into the kitchen where my cousins were playing dominoes on the floor. It was the Fourth of July, and my aunts and their husbands and children had all come over for a noon dinner. I'd eaten chicken and mashed potatoes and peas and squash and apple pie, all the while not knowing that people were looking at me and thinking that my father was a bastard. I stepped over the dominoes, dislodged a cat from the rocking chair by the window, and sat down. I could hear the TV in the living room, and pictured my uncles sprawled on the couch with the dog, groaning over their full bellies, and saying to each other, *Did you hear Steve is a bastard?* The cat stared at me spitefully. When my aunts came out of the pantry, I could feel where they were in the room without looking up.

My mother was drying dishes; her braid swung cheerfully from side to side. "You girls were talking about Steve," she said, her voice light, teasing. "You think I don't know what you're up to in there?"

"Why would we talk about Steve?" Aunt Libby said. "There are more interesting things to talk about." She began to put away the dishes my mother had dried.

"Steve will be back in fall," my mother said. "He's probably looking for a way to get rid of that woman even as we speak. He wouldn't abandon a woman in the middle of nowhere, no matter what sort of a person she is."

There was a long silence as Aunt Libby finished putting the dishes away. Then Aunt Dora said, "Of course, Honey," and Aunt Libby said, "I'm sure you're right." Only my grandmother said nothing; she finished wiping the table, then lifted me out of the rocking chair and sat down in it with me in her lap. While my mother and my aunts talked about my father, she braided and unbraided my hair. I loved the sharp smell of her skin, the deep wrinkles in her neck like a turkey's, her large breasts which she called *pillows*.

"You're my good girl, aren't you?" she said, her thick, calloused hands working in my hair.

I was in awe of my grandmother's hands. She could pull out a thistle the size of a cat without wearing gloves. She could take a platter out of the oven bare-handed. She plucked chickens and ducks without flinching, then passed their limp bodies over the gas flame on the stove to burn away the pinfeathers. One hot day, she let Alex and me follow her out to the coop, where she selected a few birds from the flock, luring them to her side by making a peculiar noise in the back of her throat. This noise, half cluck, half baby's cry, made the back of my neck feel cold despite the crushing heat.

"Not that one," Alex and I said as my grandmother patted the broad back of a chicken with a crooked flopping comb.

"You'd say that about any I picked," she said, and she tucked that chicken and another under one arm and carried them to the shed. We tagged along, excited and afraid. There she hypnotized the chickens with her hands, stroking the backs of their necks and speaking to them softly. When they'd gone into a "lovely sleep," those same hands cut their throats and hung them upside down to season overnight so they'd be "ripe" for Sunday supper.

"What happens when you make them sleep like that?" I asked. She'd killed them so quickly I hadn't had time to feel sad. One minute

9

they had been alive; now they hung from the rafters, quivering, mean-ingless as rags.

"Oh, their minds go away to someplace else," she said. "Every-thing's like a dream."

I turned to Alex, but his face wore the distant, irritated look he got whenever he thought about wolves. We walked down to our apple tree, and there he told me his newest idea: he and I were going to learn to hypnotize things. If hypnotism worked on chickens, it would prob-ably work on other kinds of animals as well. A hypnotized wolf couldn't run away; it would stay, fixed in its "lovely sleep," while Alex took samples of its fur, measured its teeth, and photographed it with the camera he'd bought for that purpose at a barn sale down the road.

Later that day, we sneaked back into the chicken coop, and, failing to lure any hens with our voices, we chased them round and round until we managed to trap one pullet behind a bag of feed. Though we moved our hands exactly the way my grandmother had, and spoke in our most soothing voices, we lacked my grandmother's magic and the pullet remained wide-eyed and outraged. When we released it, it flew to the top of the coop, battering its head against the beams. Outside, the dog was barking; we left before my grandmother came to investigate.

We attempted to hypnotize the barn cats, which hissed and ran away. We tried pigeons and snakes and one terrified rabbit; we tried the dog, Fritzie, who thumped his tail agreeably. The cows seemed permanently hypnotized; nothing we could do or say disturbed their steady gaze. We realized we were running out of subjects.

"I guess we should practice on each other first," Alex said. I was tired of hypnosis, but his face was pinched with disappointment: it was a look he wore just before he picked a fight or disappeared to cry. So I followed him into the forbidden cornfield and let him stretch out between the rows with his head in my lap. I stroked his forehead, flexing my hands the way my grandmother did, and after a while I found my thoughts contracting until they were nothing more than a speck on a wide white page. I looked down at Alex's face, and I realized by his wide-eyed silence that he was hypnotized.

"How do you feel?" I whispered.

"I feel good."

"What's it like?"

"Lovely sleep."

"Where are you?"

Alex didn't answer. I became afraid, and then my thoughts opened up and filled the space in my mind until the wideness of it all was gone.

"You will wake up on the count of three," I said quickly, because I had heard that somewhere before. "One. Two. Three."

Alex opened his eyes and sat up. He stared at me, blinked.

"I saw them," he said. "I saw the wolves. There were lots of them. They ran past me. I could feel them brushing against my legs."

"We better go," I said. "Mom will be wondering where we are."

"I *saw* them!" Alex said. "They're the most beautiful things, with silver in their tails."

"We better go," I said again. I could tell the sun was setting by the fierce gold light which made our faces and hands seem to glow. Abruptly, we heard my mother calling our names, stretching each syllable into a desperate wail. We jumped to our feet and thrashed through the stalks, frightened by the terror in her voice, and burst out of the field just ten feet from she stood. She screamed, then started to cry.

"Don't you ever do that to me," she said. "Don't you *ever*!"

"Honey, what is it?" my grandmother called, hurrying down from the house.

For our punishment, we had to eat in the basement, and then stay there until it was time for bed. To pass the time, we explored the bins in the root cellar, and we opened the door to the winter pantry and examined the old jars of home-canned fruits and vegetables. *1961*, the labels said. *1958*, *1949*. It was impossible to tell what the contents had been. Some of them were oozing brown liquid; the smell made us gasp and we put them back quickly. I sat on the stairs and tried to collapse my thoughts until they were just a speck, so that wide white space would open up again in my mind. But it wouldn't happen; I was cold and bored and tired.

That night, I woke up screaming, for in my dream I'd seen not my fingers, but Gerta Bruch's. They smelled like the liquid oozing from the old jars. They were resting on two wide squares of white linen, the shattered ends bright with blood.

We said the Rosary aloud on Wednesday nights. Aunt Dora came with Uncle Chester and their children, Paul, Stacy, and Lynn. The adults began each Hail Mary; the children completed it. *Holy Mary. Mother of God. Pray for us sinners.* I squeezed my folded hands tightly, the tips of each of my pinkies covering the scar on the opposite hand. Sometimes, days would pass when I wouldn't think about God, but on Wednesday nights, I saw myself for what I was: a flawed little girl with an imperfect soul, someone who could not go to Heaven.

Alex and my cousins fidgeted, scrunching up their faces when no one was looking, picking their noses, trying to make each other laugh. "TZZZ!" Aunt Dora would say; sometimes one of them would be sent from the room. After the Rosary was finished, my grandmother served coffee and kuchen. Often, she gave me the biggest piece and an extra teaspoon of sugar in my coffee, telling the others what a good girl I had been. My cousins, and even Alex sometimes, teased me about my piety. Once, when I went to the bathroom, they huddled outside the door chanting, *Mary, Mother of God, pee for us,* and I cried because I thought God might get confused and think it was me saying that.

I had four cousins in all. Three were Aunt Dora and Uncle Chester's; one was Aunt Libby and Uncle John's. Aunt Libby originally had had four children, but three were killed in a car accident, the same accident in which Uncle John lost his leg. He wore a wooden leg now, and he liked to dare us to step on it. "Go on," he'd say. "You can stomp it if you want," and he'd thump it with his cane, demonstrating. But we prodded it instead, tenderly, not quite believing that his own limb wasn't inside.

Aunt Libby and Uncle John never stopped by on Wednesday nights. After the accident, they had *lost their faith,* which, according to my mother, was the most terrible thing that could happen to anyone.

"How can you lose faith?" I asked, and my mother told me she didn't know, but that it was a question I should never ask Aunt Libby, because it would only make her sad. Occasionally, my mother and Aunt Dora tried to reason with Aunt Libby, but Aunt Libby was finished with *God and all His nonsense;* I heard her say that late one night when I was supposed to be asleep, and the phrase stuck in my mind as the most outrageous thing I'd ever heard anyone say.

One Wednesday night in August, Aunt Libby showed up alone. We had finished the Rosary and were sitting in the kitchen: my mother and Alex and I, my grandmother, Aunt Dora and Uncle Chester, and their children.

"Libby," my grandmother said warmly. "Next time come a little sooner."

She set a plateful of apfelkuchen in front of Aunt Libby, who frowned, and picked at it with her fork as though it was something she didn't think she should put in her mouth. Then she looked hard at my mother.

"Have you heard from Steve?"

Everyone looked at her, even Lynn, the youngest child.

"Why, no," my mother said. "But this fall . . . "

"What are you going to do?" Aunt Libby said. "When he doesn't come back, what are you going to do?"

"Libby!" Aunt Dora said.

"I know of a job," Aunt Libby said. "You're going to need a job. They're hiring fall temporaries at the canning company. I'll go with you, if you want."

"Steve will be back," my mother said, laughing a little, color rising in her face. "You don't understand."

Aunt Libby stood up. "Who do you think you are," she said, "that you think bad things can't happen to you?" She leaned across the table, her face close to my mother's face. "Damn it, Joanne. Who do you think you are?"

The phone began to ring. It was an old phone, black, mounted high up on the wall so the children couldn't reach it. It rang in a shrill, scolding voice: five rings, six, seven. I knew that we all were counting, and when the ringing finally stopped, no one knew what to do next.

"You don't know anything," my mother finally said. I expected her to cry; she always cried, easily and freely, while someone ran for a tissue. But instead she got up and went into the room she shared with my grandmother, closing the door softly but firmly behind, and it was Aunt Libby who cried.

I got up and went outside, dragging my bare feet through the wet grass, until I stood at the edge of the lawn where the cornfield began. The moon was full and pure and bright. I rarely thought about my father; he had always been away a lot, at work, or with friends, or on business trips, and so it seemed unusual to me when my mother asked if I missed him. I knew that I should miss him, and I always said that I did. But that night I knew, staring out into the corn, that I didn't care if he never came back. I turned and saw Alex behind me, his pale hair shining like a beacon.

"I've been out here at night before," he said. "But never in the field. Wolves are nocturnal animals, and they eat and drink at night, and they do all their thinking at night."

"I know," I said. "You've told me."

"Let's go in," he said, and we stepped into the field together, one row apart, and when the lights from the house disappeared behind us, we kept on walking. I knew that as long as we stayed in our row, we'd be able to find our way home, but after a while the rows became uncertain.

"We have to go back," I said. We had come to a wall of leaves, sticky and sweet smelling, catching in our hair. Abruptly the corn came alive with whispers. The sound swelled as if fed by the moon, growing louder and stronger until it shook the leaves all around us.

"Look!" Alex said, and they were running past us, fleet footed and silver, brushing our legs, panting, filling the air with their scent: rank, bitter, wild. They held their shoulders high, their tails low; they sniffed us like farm dogs and passed us by, wrestling, snapping, crashing between the corn rows. In the clear light of the moon I saw collars hanging from the necks of two.

For a moment, we stared after them, but the corn had swallowed them up and there was nothing left to see.

"Dogs," Alex said quietly.

"What do you mean?" I said.

"They had collars. They were dogs."

"I didn't see any collars."

"I thought they had collars," Alex said.

"No, they didn't."

For a long time we stood silently, hoping they would return. We looked for them every day for the rest of the summer, but we never saw them again, and at the end of August, my father came to take us home.

Detroit that fall was terrible and cold. My father spoke often of California, and he sat up drinking late into the night, remembering warmer places. I started middle school, and sometimes, seeing Alex in the halls, I stared at him like he was someone I'd never seen before, a tall skinny boy with an earring and spiked hair, his face always angry and his pale hair turning brown. He did not care about wolves anymore; he seemed to have forgotten the summer. When he spoke of my

grandmother, he called her *that old woman;* when he spoke of my
mother, he used no name at all.

My father disappeared again just after Christmas, and my mother,
in her new hard way, found a day job in a department store, and at
night, took classes to become a dental hygienist.

"You and Alex are old enough to look out for each other," she said,
and though I didn't think I was old enough at all, I knew that what I
thought made no difference anymore. My mother was doing what
had to be done; at night, while she was in school, and Alex roamed the
streets with friends, I opened up my mind to that wide, white space,
and let myself drift away.

I still had dreams about my fingers, but the dreams were not as
terrible as they once had been. The few times I awoke in tears and
tried getting into bed with my mother, she told me I was too old for
all that. "Turn on a light if you feel afraid," she said. Her eyes were
sunken; she had cut her pretty hair. She was tired from working and
going to school; still, when the letters started coming from my father,
she dropped them down the garbage disposal without reading them.
From the expression on her face, it was easy for me to imagine that she
was stuffing *him* down that awful hole, and part of me felt gleeful and
wicked, and part of me felt sad.

He came back to visit one last time. It was a Saturday, early the
following spring, and he was supposed to take Alex and me to a
restaurant. But Alex would have nothing to do with it, and, when my
father arrived, I was all alone. My mother was studying at a friend's
house. My father seemed relieved.

"I guess it's just the two of us," he said, and he tucked and retucked
his shirt into his pants, something he always did when he wasn't sure
what to do next. He seemed to have forgotten about the restaurant;
we drove around the suburbs instead. My father slowed in front of
the houses he particularly liked, studying the toys scattered on the
sidewalks, the flower gardens bright with crocuses and daffodils, the
wooden ducks and geese and sheep nestled in the shrubs.

"I been thinking I might move to a trailer park," he said after a while. "They got these parks down in Florida just for old farts like me."

I was nauseous from driving and from missing lunch. I didn't feel I knew him well enough to say I wanted to go home.

"Those parks," he said, "you move into one of them and bingo! You got neighbors, good neighbors. Neighbors are important," he said, and he slowed in front of another house, a long low brick ranch. "Look at this one," he said, "now isn't it a beauty?"

I stared at the house which, to me, looked no different than any of the others we had seen. It was bigger than our house, which we rented. The lawn was neatly mowed, the sidewalk swept white. Someone had pasted a crayon drawing of a large blue and white striped cat in the front bay window.

"How big a family you think lives here?" he said. "Four kids? Five?"

"Five," I said, to say something.

"Yeah," my father said. "Five kids, can you imagine it?"

I shook my head.

"I always look at people like that," he said, "and I wonder how can they do it? Because I wanted to be that way. All my life," he said, "that's what I've really wanted."

"Can we go home now?" I said, and the sudden hurt look that sharpened his face made me angry, so angry that I had to look away. I didn't like any of the houses he had shown me; I didn't dislike them either. I didn't understand what he wanted me to say. I felt like I did at school, dull witted and shy, unable to guess the right answer no matter how much the teacher prompted.

"Okay, Sweetheart," he said.

We drove back home without saying anything. When we got to our house with its ragged yard, the gray paint peeling off the front porch, my father sighed. The hedge had grown wide, spilling across the sidewalk. The windows were empty, except for plain white curtains; there were no toys, no flowers, no sign that anyone lived there.

"I guess you're glad to be home," he said, and I said, Yes I was. He came in, briefly, to use the bathroom. I waited for him in the living room, listening to the faint sound of him whistling under his breath, and trying to remember that sound because I knew it would be the last time I'd hear it. When he came out, he hugged me stiffly; I tried not to pull away.

"You can come visit me in Florida, how would you like that?" he said.

"Great!" I said, trying to sound like I meant it, but really just wanting him to go.

"Okay," he said. He was anxious to go, too. I waved to him from the doorway until he was out of sight; only then did I wish he had not left so soon. I went to my room and lay down on my bed. I tried to imagine Florida, but as it turned out, he didn't go there at all, but to Montana, and after that, Canada, and after that, Kansas, Idaho, Maine, and many, many places after that until, finally, nobody knew.

Eliza awakens to his breath upon her forehead. She does not open her eyes. The weight of him is like water, moist and warm. There are sounds; the clatter of maple branches against the window, the winter wind beneath the front door humming like breath blown across an open bottle. But the dead man himself is silent. When she opens her eyes, he disappears.

The green eyes of Michael Gabriel glow like clocks in the darkness. He is the oldest of Eliza's cats, the wisest, she thinks, the most beautiful. He picks his way across the clenched fist of her body, settles beside her cheek, begins to purr. She pinches the cool tips of his ears lightly between her fingers; she will not be deceived. For the air holds the clean, cold scent of smoke, the smell of the heavy overcoat Andrew wore last fall when he went out back to burn the leaves and his heart split like dry pine.

Michael Gabriel's ribs are smooth; hard beneath Eliza's hand. She kisses him and rattles the box of cat treats she keeps beside the bed. John Paul floats up from the floor, nips a treat from her hand. Cecilia Marie settles soft against her thigh. Andrew always hated cats, their sleek, snake bodies, their cunning. *A waste of an animal,* he said, *a crying mouth, and what do you get after you feed it?*

She was certain he wouldn't come back to a house full of cats. But nights she hears the smoke drifting across the cold floors. It lingers in the corners of the house during the day, seeps in beneath the windows.

Eliza works her arms out from under the quilts and decorates herself with the limp, warm bodies of the cats. An hour passes. The dark thins. The smell of smoke slips from the air.

By mid-morning, gray light filters through the heavy frost angels on the window. Eliza sees her breath. She pulls herself into sitting position, swings her legs stiffly over the side of the bed. The cats stretch, their toes kneading the air, and none of them opens their eyes. The hollows in their cheeks reveal their pointed teeth.

Eliza takes her clothes into the bathroom to dress, a habit from when Andrew was alive. She doesn't put in her teeth; there is ice around the glass where they have soaked for almost three months. But she washes her face and hands and brushes her tight, gray curls and rubs her neck with Vicks to ward off cold.

Then she goes into the living room and turns on the TV. While it warms up, she makes instant coffee and fills her mouth with soda crackers. She holds the crackers between her gums and swallows the coffee over them to make them soft.

The TV blares. Eliza burrows beneath the afghan on the couch to watch what's left of the morning programs, the coffee cup tucked warm into her palm. John Paul comes out of the bedroom, yawns, hops nimbly onto her lap. He coughs, a dry, ragged sound; Eliza sniffs the air.

Polly Fischer arrives at half past noon. Polly is forty-five and a volunteer for Meals on Wheels. She brings Eliza and people like Eliza a hot meal once a day. Eliza is amazed that a woman Polly's age can look so old.

"WE HAVE CHILI," says Polly. "WE HAVE CORN BREAD. WE HAVE PEAS."

Polly wears bright pink lipstick and a pink sweatshirt to match. Around the collar of the sweatshirt are white, fleecy lambs, and the fleecy part sticks up off the shirt. The cats skulk behind the furniture. They work their noses hard at the smell of Polly's perfume.

Polly sits with Eliza while she eats. Together they watch "Days of Our Lives." Polly stops talking during the kissing scenes and stares outright at the screen.

"I COULD USE SOME OF THAT," Polly says.

Eliza says, "You are much better off without it."

"YOU OKAY?" Polly says. "YOU LOOK AWFUL TIRED, HON."

"My husband has been pestering me," Eliza says. "If it wasn't for my kitties, I'd never get no sleep."

"ANIMALS CAN BE SUCH A COMFORT."

"He just won't let me be."

"YOU SHOULD GET YOURSELF A DOG. BE SAFER, LIVING OUT HERE ALL ALONE."

"Why, that would be silly. My husband loved dogs. It's my kitties what keep him away."

"GOD REST HIS SOUL," Polly says.

4

At dusk, Eliza hears Andrew in the bathroom, flipping through the pages of the *Popular Mechanics* she threw out after his death. She goes to the refrigerator and opens the leftovers that Polly has wrapped carefully in foil. Eliza takes two mouthfuls of the chili and swallows the rest of the peas. The cats swarm around her legs, knocking their heads into her ankles. She sets the rest of the chili on the floor. The cats' heads crowd together over the plastic tray. They eat ferociously, tails snapping. Eliza keeps her eyes on the bathroom door.

What do you want? she says.

There is a long silence from the bathroom, so thick, so white with emptiness, that Eliza falls back against the smooth cold surface of the counter.

Then, the sound of pages turning, *flip, flip*. The cats wash their whiskers. They keep their eyes on Eliza: eyes that glitter, hungry for more.

He wakes her just before dawn. She sees the smudge of his shadow in the corner across from her bed. She calls to the cats, rattles the box of treats. The cats cluster in the doorway, but none of them will come in. Michael Gabriel's green eyes narrow into crescent moons. John Paul chokes on the smokey air.

The hens need feeding, Andrew says.

I don't keep hens no more.

The cow.

Cow's gone.

You got to milk regular or it cramps up their tits.

The shadow unfolds. It is round like a wide wailing mouth.

There is no milk. There is no butter.

Andrew.

I can't abide this, Andrew says.

Andrew's hands are wood colored, stained with grease, but smooth—so smooth!—to the touch. His cows are clean and well cared for, and he names them all, up to eighteen in the good years, and remembers their names. Month after month, Eliza swallows the bitter herbs his mother prepares even after it is certain no child will come of it, and all because of his sweet way with those cows, and how he keeps his hands for them.

Eliza is long boned, broad shouldered and strong; she works side by side with him and never once holds him back. She keeps her house clean and the pantry stocked with what she brings in from her garden. And she cooks; she is a good cook, she got that from her mother.

At supper she feeds him ham and scalloped potatoes, creamed corn, beans, bread with butter and sugar, apple sauce and relish, and thick wedges of pie.

You want anything more? she says. Just tell me what you want.

Gawd, he says, I can't eat another mouthful.

But at night he creeps to the kitchen and gorges on leftovers, bread and jam, cream skimmed from the pitcher. She lies awake listening to the careful sounds, the muffled clang of a pot lid, the heavy creak of the pantry door. Yet, in the morning his stomach rages, quivering as though he is heavy with child.

And she rises and whips up pancakes, scrambled eggs and bacon, toast and spiced pears and fried potatoes, and when she sets the platter before him she might even risk a shy kiss to his forehead.

But it is never enough. He eats silently, scraping his plate. When he catches her staring, she lowers her head.

You about ready? he finally says. We better get to it, then, we got a lot to do.

His eyes still on the last strip of bacon. That heavy belly cupped beneath his hands.

7

Smoke hangs thick in the air when Eliza awakens. She dresses and tugs on her worn wool coat, the lining hanging about the hem like lace. She winds a scarf around her head and walks half a mile up the road to the Petersons'.

Jenny Peterson fixes her up with hot coffee, oatmeal, and a mason jar of Tang. Eliza tries to eat, but her stomach feels the size of a walnut inside her.

"You just missed Earl and the kids," Jenny says.

Eliza sips at her coffee, the only thing that tastes good to her.

"I feel bad you walked all the way over here," Jenny says. "I keep meaning to stop by to get your shopping list. I was going to have Earl stop by last night, now I'm kicking myself I didn't."

"It's just I am out of everything," Eliza says. "I am sorry to bother you about it."

"It's no bother, now you know that."

"I need bread and jam and sody crackers and food for my kitties. I need soap. And maybe some tuna."

23

"We'll fix you up."

"You will not believe what is happening," Eliza says. "It's Andrew. He won't give me no peace."

"Andrew?"

"Last night he was in the bathroom. And he came to sit by my bed."

Jenny bites deep into a slice of toast. "Are you sure it's him?"

"It's him."

"Well, think about it," Jenny says. "You must've done something to disturb his rest."

"I can't think what that would be."

"Or there's things unresolved between you. That's how it was with Ma and me."

"I cannot remember," Eliza says. "We were married for fifty-one years."

"There must be something, then," Jenny says.

8

Always he is hungry. At night he braids his fingers through her hair, spreads her legs with quick thrusts of his knees. She would do whatever he asks of her, but Andrew never asks much, so she waits beneath him until he pats her cheek to let her know he is finished.

During the night he slips out from beneath the quilts, comes back with a chunk of bread spread thick with cheese, a handful of cookies. How her mouth waters for that cheese! but she refuses to taste it. He eats that cheese by himself and licks his own fingers when he finishes.

She could have refused the marriage. *If you don't suit each other, there's no sense to it,* her father said. She and Andrew were married on a clear, cold October day, and everyone said the weather was God's blessing. She carried a bunch of marigolds that left her hands pungent and green. That night, as Andrew slept, his belly skin stretched tight with cake and apple wine, she lay awake smelling her fingers.

Jenny walks Eliza out to Earl's old truck.

"I don't know how you walk so far," Jenny says.

"I don't know either," Eliza says. "I can't say I ever enjoyed it."

"It's great, now that Earl got the Chevy," Jenny says. "Now I can go anywhere I please."

"It must be nice," Eliza says.

"It's heaven," Jenny says.

Jenny drives Eliza into town for her groceries. Eliza is short three dollars and Jenny pays the difference. Then Jenny loads the bag between them in the truck and drives Eliza home. Grainy bits of snow whirl through the air. When Eliza opens the front door, the cats skitter in all directions. Jenny raises her eyebrows.

"You know, these cats eat more than you," she says. "I'd be happy to take them for you. We always get a ton of mice in winter."

"They don't eat so much."

"You know, cats tempt the dead."

Eliza reaches down to pat Michael Gabriel. He ducks his head, dashes away. His green eyes flash with disdain.

"That one," Jenny says. "He has got such lovely eyes. I could get use to eyes like that."

"All you do for me," says Eliza. "God knows I appreciate it."

"And that sick one," Jenny says. "You should let me take it, I'd get it to a vet, I would do that."

"God knows I do."

"You'd see them when you wanted. I could feed them proper, you know they are hungry."

"I feed them proper. All you do for me."

"The green-eyed one and the sick one." Jenny points to John Paul. "You can keep the other one."

"But they are mine," Eliza says. Her stomach burns.

Jenny takes them out to the truck, one at a time. They hiss, twisting in her hands, whipping their tails through the air like rope. Eliza cannot watch. Even so, when she hears the truck bounce down the drive, she opens the door just enough to slip out her hand to wave.

Cecilia Marie hurtles through the opening and bounds across the ice crust to the barn. Eliza calls for her over and over, but she does not come back. Smoke scratches the walls and Eliza burrows beneath the afghan, listening.

"**W**HAT A SMELL," says Polly Fischer when she brings Eliza her noon meal.

"It's Andrew," Eliza says.

"I'LL BRING ALONG SOME AIR FRESHENER NEXT TIME I COME. I GOT SOME LOVELY LILAC SPRAY."

"She has my kitties," Eliza says. "Now there's nothing to keep him away."

"LILACS ALWAYS REMIND ME OF SOMETHING."

"You get attached to kitties. You get to know their ways."

"HOW COME I DON'T SEE YOUR KITTY-CATS, HON?"

"The one I got left, she slipped out. My little one. I had her from a kitten."

After "Days of Our Lives," Polly trudges round the barn and calls for Cecilia Marie. Eliza hears her voice like a whistle, high and clear on the wind. It is not a voice that draws you near. It is not a voice you trust.

By dusk, the house is blue with smoke. Eliza is crazy with the waiting. She circles the couch, drinking cup after cup of instant coffee, pressing her fingers between her gums. When he brushes past her, she is relieved. He moves from room to room and she trails behind him as though they are newly married and she is trying desperately, desperately to know how she must be to please him. Can I get you something? she says. Tell me what I can do.

Fresh corn, he says. *Asparagus.*

What is it?

Potatoes. Gravy. Salt.

What?

Dumplings with cream sauce.

The shadow of him lashes the walls. She can smell his breath, faint and human, drifting beneath the smoke. He has spent the morning raking. He has the leaves in two big piles, burning at the edge of the lawn where the beet field begins. The wind switches abruptly. Smoke billows against the windows of the house, colors the air. She goes out to warn him. She has always been terrified of fire. And when she calls his name he pitches forward into the flames.

She thought for weeks she'd somehow killed him, even after they explained to her the strange and fragile workings of his heart. What did she know about hearts? They talked about cholesterol, poor diet, weakness. It took all her strength to pull him from the leaves by the feet, her fingernails digging into his thick rubber galoshes. She put out the fire in his collar with her hands, gagging on the smell of his bright, blistered head, glowing free of hair, rough with clots of ash and blisters that rose and whitened even as he died.

Baked ham with pineapple, he says. *Sauerkraut and sausage.*

What do you want from me? she says. Andrew, Andrew.

Night comes on as she remembers. How she screamed his name into his ears. He died with his eyes open wide as they could go, yet not even then did he recognize her.

Ohio

for Steve Williams

I t was still dark when Stuart carried his suitcase out to the car. The street lights glowed in single file up and down the block, and it seemed to him that their slender necks were bending beneath the weight of each bulb. He breathed deeply, and the feeling reminded him of church and afterward, when you walked outside into the bright Sunday morning and knew you were capable of only good things. A small shape floated across the windshield and onto the hood of the car. A leaf, he thought, but when he touched it his fingers sank into the soft startled wetness of a frog. He drew back and wiped his hand on his jeans. Now he could hear a few birds twittering in the bushes, and the sound was like whispers, like the snickering of girls at school.

In the house, his mother was leaning over the cluttered bathroom sink, pressing rouge to her cheeks with a special round pad. She had told him to dress simply: worn jeans, sneakers, and a T-shirt. This, she had explained, was what his father would be wearing. But she had risen two hours earlier to put on a dress and fix her hair. Tiny gold crosses glittered from her ears.

"You about ready?" Stuart asked, trying not to sound impatient, because if he did, it would make her take even longer.

"My bags are in the kitchen," she said without moving her mouth. "You can take them on out, I'll be right there." She puffed up her cheeks, dabbed more rouge onto the pad. He noticed how her shoulders poked forward beneath her thin, cotton dress, and he wished she would put on a sweater; he wished she would be more careful when she drove, and that she would take vitamins regularly. She was the only person he had ever loved, and he worried that God would take her from him. Stuart was fourteen, and he was afraid that he loved his mother too much.

Outside, he sensed a difference in the air, like a whiff of an almost-familiar scent, that meant night had changed into early morning. He arranged his mother's suitcases beside his own and slammed the trunk, hoping she would hear the sound and understand how ready he was to go. He had only been out of Maine twice before, and that was just to New Hampshire, and he thought he couldn't bear to stay in this state, in this town, in this cramped, gray yard, for one moment longer. Mosquitoes descended on him then, and though he couldn't see them, he heard their insistent whining, felt their wings brush against his arms and neck. He got in the car and closed the door and pulled his seatbelt over his lap, and by the time he looked up, his mother was coming, moving sleek and steady as a cat. She did not wear shoes with less than a three-inch heel, yet her feet always hit the ground squarely when she walked. She sounded like a ticking clock.

Before he'd been born, before she'd married his father, Stuart's mother hadn't taken any pride in her appearance. *I didn't bother to keep myself up*, she'd told him on the eve of her thirtieth birthday, curling her fingers to examine the fresh plum coat on her nails. They were sitting on the front steps, the uncut cake between them—chocolate, with butter-creme swirls. Stuart's mother struck a match off her thumb nail; she repeated the act until Stuart could do it too, and then she clapped as his flame licked the tops of the candles, one by one. Across the street, the neighbor's dogs stopped pacing the chain-link fence that enclosed them and stared, panting, at the quiet burst of light. Later that evening, she showed him the photographs she'd kept, she said, *so that I'll never forget.* In each one she looked more painfully thin, her hair lackluster and matted like fur, her breasts no more than a wrinkle, her mouth a wide, angry curve. *I put anything into my body, then,* she told him. *Drugs, men. It didn't matter.* Stuart was ten, and he believed he understood exactly what she meant.

Now, when she opened the car door, a dozen metal bracelets quarreled on her wrists. She was capable looking, and pretty, the head secretary and receptionist at their church. "If you're nervous," she told Stuart, lifting her long legs into the car, "don't be."

"I'm not," he said, but he knew she wouldn't believe him. Stuart could not even remember what his father looked like. Ten years ago, his father had abandoned Stuart and his mother along with the Church of Christ's Love where he was junior pastor, and, except for sporadic child support, they hadn't heard from him in a long time. Now he had written to say that he wanted to put things right. He had gone back to school and was living with a woman from Ohio. Though he realized the union wasn't legal, he considered himself *married in his heart* and he wanted Stuart to think of Miriam as his stepmother, and their little girl, Mars, as his sister. He hoped Stuart's mother would understand that, though God was no longer a part of his life, he respected her beliefs and, if Stuart were to visit, would do nothing to contradict them. This was the reason Stuart's mother was driving him all the way to Massachusetts, to the old farmhouse his father and Miriam were fixing up themselves. Stuart was to win his father's heart back to Christ. His mother would continue on to New York State, where she'd stay with her old friend Emily, but she would return to pick him up at the end of the visit, which was supposed to last a week.

It was the little girl, Stuart's mother said, who she felt the most sorry for. Poor thing, raised by hippies, not even given the comfort of a Christian name. *That's how it was for me,* she said. *I knew nothing of God's love.* Stuart imagined Mars as an ashen-faced, wispy child, her eyes deep with longing. When she saw him for the first time she would stand up very slowly and walk over to him step by jolting step, drawn by the gossamer fingers of the Holy Spirit. He would baptize her right on the spot with water from the vial he'd hidden in his pocket, and she'd lick the droplets from around her mouth greedily, a traveler just emerging from a wide and terrible desert.

But actually, Stuart wasn't sure what to expect. It would be the first time he had witnessed alone, and as they pulled out of the driveway, he felt that he was about to be changed in some mysterious and unalterable way. It was a feeling he had frequently, though nothing ever seemed to happen as a result. His mother said it was God tapping lightly on his shoulder, a test to see if he was listening, to see what he would do if truly called. The feeling, she said, meant that Stuart had grace, but Stuart suspected he had only emptiness, and this was his most shameful secret. He saw his life as a series of complex imitations, all of which were performed exactingly, but without understanding. And like any imposter, he was afraid of being exposed only slightly more than he was afraid he would never be discovered.

His mother flicked on the radio. "Who's my best sweetheart?" she asked.

"I am," he said automatically. They were heading south on 95, the humped shoulders of the pine forests beginning to glisten as the sun rose over the ocean. Gulls drifted high above them, singly, calling as if they were lost. Crossing the bridge from Maine into New Hampshire, the interstate lights winked out in waves, and for a while Stuart and his mother kept pace, reaching each new section of lights just in time to watch them fade from gold to white.

When they had driven as far as the Massachusetts turnpike, they pulled off at a rest area to get something to eat. The sun had burned away the morning haze and now, in the heat, the interstate traffic sounded angry and huge, like a single soulless creature. It was difficult to imagine that each car was driven by an individual person, that each person was driving for a specific reason to a specific place where there would be more individual people, each with lives of their own. Stuart was afraid he would never have enough love in his heart to encompass them all, and for this he would be held accountable. He felt an overwhelming sense of claustrophobia, walking beside his mother into the restaurant, standing in line to order burgers and sodas and salty fries.

"It's strange to be away on a Saturday," his mother said, wrestling napkins from the dispenser on the counter. "It doesn't feel right somehow."

Every summer since Stuart could remember, they had spent Saturday afternoons with other members of the Church of Christ's Love congregation, going from door to door and neighborhood to neighborhood, inviting people to come to Sunday services. They canvased Portland and the surrounding, smaller towns: Saco, Old Orchard Beach, Biddeford, Gorham. Before going out on the route Pastor Hardy set for them, they'd meet at somebody's house for potluck and rich, creamy desserts. Afterward, they'd form a Circle of Prayer, joining hands and asking God to help them to be His messengers, His voice on earth. Sometimes, individual members would ask for a specific intention. Stuart asked again and again that God help him not to feel embarrassed, especially when somebody his own age answered the door, especially when it was someone he recognized from school. He knew he should make his petition out loud, but he was afraid of hurting his mother, for this was something she believed he still enjoyed the way he did when he was five and six and seven, still clinging to her hand.

And it had been fun, riding in the back of the van with the other children, tumbling out of the double doors and racing up the street ahead of the adults to tell them if it looked like anyone was home. At the door, the smallest child would be lifted up to ring the bell while the others held the slippery stacks of pamphlets, smiling brightly. *Show your joy,* Pastor Hardy said, for faith was a lit candle, something that should shine for all to see. Stuart and the other children tried their best to act joyful while the adults spoke in low, polite voices to the person who answered the door. If that person were a woman, the women in the group spoke first, putting her at ease, making it clear they were mothers themselves, the sort of people you could open your door to without fear. If the person who answered the door was a man, then the men in the group stepped forward, their arms bent into crisp right angles, because often a man would shake hands automatically, and after shaking hands with someone, it becomes more difficult to turn them away.

Stuart ate his burgers quickly, and then he watched his mother as she nibbled the tips of her fries, stuffing them back, half-eaten, into the package if they weren't perfectly crispy. She made Stuart laugh by twisting the paper wrapper at one end of her soda straw and blowing through the other. The wrapper shot off the straw and hit him in the chest. "Bull's eye," she said, and he reached for his own straw, but he'd already removed the wrapper and scrunched it into a ragged wad. Some little boys at the next booth were staring; Stuart's mother fluttered her fingers at them, and they ducked down behind the high orange seat. Stuart was suddenly, wildly happy. He wished he and his mother could just keep on driving forever, stopping at restaurants whenever they were hungry, camping at night beneath the wide white eyes of the stars. On the road, day after day, week after week, his life would be shaken into place until everything fit together into the snug, neat picture that was faith. Then, just the way Pastor Hardy promised, his eyes would be truly opened. He would see beyond the surface shapes of things and understand their meaning, and he would be able to love the world the way Christ's teachings required. When kids at school teased him, when girls giggled behind their hands as he passed them in the halls, he would forgive them, for he would realize that what his mother had told him was true: they were envious, bound to the world as they were. They were jealous of his faith. He should smile kindly and move on, and from now on that's exactly what he would do.

Thinking of this, he followed his mother back to the car eagerly and with great hope. But the traffic sounded the same, and the sun was uncomfortably warm, and soon they were gliding off the turnpike and into the countryside without anything having changed. Stuart closed his eyes, worrying about what he would say to his father and stepmother. He did not believe, the way his mother and Pastor Hardy believed, that the Spirit would move him to say the right things. He was afraid that all his life he would have to pretend the way the school foreign-exchange students pretended, nodding their heads in all the right places without understanding anything you said.

His mother began talking about how much she looked forward to seeing Emily, who she'd known since they were both sixteen, cutting classes at the same high school Stuart attended now. It was Emily who'd introduced Stuart's mother to his father, saying, *You ought to talk to this guy, he's crazy, he says he's going to be a preacher someday.* But now Emily was a Christian too, married to a Christian man.

"Your father had an amazing voice," his mother said. "Like music, people listened to it, listened and wanted more. It didn't even matter what he said as much as how he said it. It was a gift, like speaking in tongues, something you just heard and understood. We went for a walk and I cried for hours. He said it was the poison washing out of me."

Stuart didn't know what to say. "What's Emily like?" he finally asked.

His mother laughed. "She's a firecracker. You met her once before she moved away."

"I remember."

"You were just a baby."

"I remember it," Stuart insisted, and his mother laughed and made a face at him, but she did not contradict.

They arrived at the farmhouse early in the afternoon; Stuart's mother stopped the car at the foot of the long dirt drive. His father had written to Stuart about the meadow flowers and the tiny wandering stream and the chicks he had ordered from a catalog. Miriam, he said, had plans to keep horses. If Stuart wanted to visit he could help lay in a fence. He could hike into the Berkshires. He could stay as long as he wished. The letter was signed *Love,* instead of *In His Love,* the way his father used to sign his letters when he was junior pastor.

"Aren't you going to come in?" Stuart said, but his mother shook her head. High overhead, two hawks circled and circled as if the car below them was prey.

"I don't want to see him," she said. "You don't know what that would do to me."

"I don't want to go by myself."

"I would say terrible things if I saw that man. Things I don't want on my conscience." She leaned over and pressed her forehead to his cheek, and he smelled the medicinal odor of her hairspray. "Don't be mad with me."

"Mom," he said, and he wanted to tell her what he had told only Pastor Hardy, that he probably didn't have grace after all, that *Jesus* had become an echo of a word that he remembered but could no longer say without blasphemy. He wanted to say that he loved only her, and if she wanted him to do this, he would do it, but not for God.

"Your father gave me the most precious things I have," she said. "He gave me my faith, and he gave me you." She straightened up and got out of the car and opened up the trunk. "Now, I'm about to repay that debt."

This was even worse than what he felt as he got older, going door to door all those Saturday afternoons wearing stiff clean clothes and a smile pressed to his face and all the while wondering what was going to happen next. Mostly people just shook their heads and closed their doors, but others would tell them to go to hell, drop dead, piss off. A man showed them dirty pictures from his wallet. A couple stood in their doorway, naked and drunk and laughing. A woman ignored the adults completely and bent her heads close to the children. *Are they treating you okay?* she had asked. *Are they forcing you to do this?*

His mother kissed him on the lips for goodbye, and he tasted her stale breath. "Your father will see God's light in you," she said. "He'll come to his senses, and the woman too." She looked out over the fields, and when she spoke again Stuart recognized her church voice, the one that made you listen whether you wanted to or not, the one that made you ache to speak in tongues and prophesize until you fell into a sleep that left you still and clean and filled with grace enough to last a lifetime. He wondered for the first time if she'd learned it from his father. "God never intends for any soul to be lost," she said. "I believe He knew about this situation even before you were born, even before your dad and I got together. I believe it was always in His plan for you to come and set things right. That poor little girl, named after some planet," and then she shook her head and spoke in her normal voice again. "At least they didn't call her Pluto. Or Uranus."

In the distance, the front door of the house opened. A figure appeared, then another. One of the figures raised an arm, but both had long hair so Stuart couldn't tell which was his father. Stuart's mother did not wave back. Instead, she got into the car and started to pull away. Then she paused and inched back to where Stuart was still standing. "If it's really awful," she whispered, as if they were standing close enough to overhear, "just call me at Em's and I'll come get you right away."

"I'll be okay," Stuart said, and then he turned and walked up the drive, stepping over pot holes shining with water. Thistles were blooming in the ditches, and small birds ducked between them, a scissoring of wings. He decided he would come right out and say, Do you still accept Jesus as your Savior? No, he would just say hello. Or maybe he wouldn't say anything, he'd just wait for one of them to speak first. When he looked up again, the figures in the doorway had turned into a woman and a man, the woman standing off to the left and Stuart's father, whom he recognized after all, just behind her. He had a sudden memory of sitting on his father's lap, his back pressed into his father's stomach. It was dusk, late summer, and his father had just finished cutting the grass. A wall of fireflies moved toward them until, up close, it broke apart, the pieces dancing around them.

"You remember me, then," his father said, and he cupped Stuart's face in his hand. For a moment, Stuart wondered if his father would kiss him, perhaps on the lips, and his stomach squirmed with the awfulness of it even after his father took his hand away. He knew he should say something, say—*something*. But he could not.

"And this is Miriam," his father said, putting one arm around her broad shoulders. Looking into her face, Stuart imagined he could see the flat, midwestern landscape of her childhood laid out as plainly as the pictures in his geography book at school, the crisp cut squares of wheat and corn, the wide tornado sky in August and the dulling snow in winter that pressed everything smooth beneath it. At first, he thought she had made up her eyes in what his mother called *earth tones:* dun, moss, slate. Then he realized that this was the color of her skin. Her eyelashes were distinct and dark, the thick legs of a spider creeping close. When she leaned to kiss him he pulled away, even though his father was watching. The back of his throat was dry with the terrible obligation to be kind.

"There's no reason we should all be friends right away," his father said. The legs of Miriam's jeans rubbed against each other as she turned and led them into the house. She had a slow, scuffling way of moving, as if there was nowhere in particular she needed to be. Stuart thought of the word *slothful,* which Pastor Hardy said meant *lazy.* In Bible study he had seen photographs of a sloth, a sad blind animal, directionless, sinful.

The house was big and breezy inside, three times the size of Stuart's own house, and cluttered with toys, coffee cups, newspapers, and magazines on astrology, child care, horses. A star chart hung high on the living-room wall, and crystals spun colored lights from the windows. Lining the low stone hearth in front of the fireplace was a military row of stuffed animals, and their black eyes glittered at Stuart as if they were waiting to pounce. "We'll get you something to drink, first," his father was saying, and though Stuart wasn't really thirsty, he was relieved to have a clear indication of what he was supposed to do next. The house had many oddly shaped rooms, and he peeked into each of them as he passed by, but didn't see the little girl, Mars.

"So how's your mother?" his father asked when he and Stuart were seated at the kitchen table. Stuart suddenly wished he had remembered to shake his father's hand. He wanted his father to see how old he'd grown, how manly. He wanted him to regret, deeply, everything he'd missed.

"Fine."

Miriam was fixing tall glasses of instant iced tea, stirring each one with her long middle finger. All of her fingernails were bitten to the quick. She was plain, and her skin was bright with oil; she looked nothing like Stuart's mother. When she brought the glasses of iced tea to the table, she added a spoonful of sugar to each from the sugar bowl in the center of the table. Then she added three more spoonfuls to her own. "I like mine sweet," she said, and she looked squarely at Stuart for the first time, as if she expected him to contradict.

"Do you still go to church?" he blurted to no one in particular, and then he felt his blush creep up his neck.

"Here we go," Miriam said. "He's going to be after us all week long," but his father shook his head at her, his eyes pleading.

"Gwen told him to say that," he said, and then to Stuart, "Your mother told you to say that, right?"

"I guess," he said. Too late, he thought of the right answer; *God told me to say it.* But the moment had passed, and his father was pushing his chair back from the table.

"Well, now you've got it over with," he said. "You did what you were supposed to do, so there's nothing to feel guilty about. I remember how all that was."

Stuart didn't know what to say.

"Do you want to get to work on that fence?" He carried his and Stuart's half-filled iced tea glasses over to the sink. "There's nothing like hard work to get to know somebody better."

"*Stuart,*" Miriam said, like she was tasting the word, and it needed something. "Is that a religious name?"

"It's Gwen's maiden name," his father said.

"It sounds so formal," Miriam said as if Stuart wasn't even there, and she added another spoonful of sugar to her own iced tea. "By the time you get back, Mars should be up from her nap."

"Is Mars *your* maiden name?" Stuart said. Miriam blinked at him, then laughed a big, bold pleasant laugh that made Stuart understand he'd done the right thing, though he did not understand why.

"Mars was named for her birth sign, and it suits her to a T," she said. "You'll see what I mean when you meet her. All she's talked about for days is her new big brother."

The black flies were covering Stuart's neck and face and the backs of his hands by the time he and his father reached the edge of the pasture, following the wide trail of flattened grass that ended at the pile of rough posts. "I hauled these out yesterday," his father said. "We might as well start here," and he dropped the bundle of tools he had been carrying, balanced across his shoulder as easily as a child. There was a pickaxe, a spade, a thick metal crowbar, and something that looked to Stuart like two shovels fastened together. He picked it up, squeezing the handles so the shovels snapped together like jaws.

"That's a clamshell," his father said. "It brings the dirt up out of the hole."

Stuart stabbed the clamshell fiercely at the sod, and it bounced back up, nicking his shin. He could feel his face darken; his eyes watered and stung. Far back in his mind, he could hear the tips of the grasses scratching at the knees of his jeans.

"There's a trick to it," his father said kindly, "like everything else in life, huh?" and he scratched away a patch of the grassy carpet with the spade, then handed Stuart the pickaxe. "Let gravity guide the point down," he said. "If you use too much muscle, you'll wind up catching your foot."

The pickaxe was evil looking, a tool the devil might carry, and lifting it made Stuart feel like someone he did not know. But it was good to hear the point rip through the sod, puncturing the rocky soil below. "Attaboy!" his father said, and he moved in to clear away the loosed dirt with his spade. "Give it another whack," and Stuart attacked the ground again, gradually growing comfortable with the weight of the axe, the way it felt in his hands.

They took turns, and Stuart glanced up now and then at the sloping hills around the fields, charting the progress of the long shadows that slid toward him like reaching fingers. The hills were the beginnings of the Berkshires; you couldn't tell what was behind them. He tried to imagine how it would be to grow up in a place like Ohio, so flat that your shadow bled away from you in perfect proportion, and you saw what was coming toward you miles before it got there. In such a place, you would never be disillusioned or surprised. If there was a God, He would be visible. There'd be nowhere for Him to hide.

He was breathing hard and so was his father. Each hole had to be three feet deep, and it took both of them to work the clamshell, heavy with rocks and dirt. His hands were blistering. He could smell his father's sweat and an oniony odor which he realized was his own, and when they took breaks they drank from the same bottle of water, not bothering to wipe off the mouth. Stuart began to tell his father about school and his mother and the people they knew from church. His father told him things about his own life with Miriam and Mars, and Stuart did not realize how much they had been talking until his voice grew hoarse and began to crack. Then he realized that this had nothing to do with what he was supposed to be talking about. He thought about his mother, who by now must be with Emily, and how the two of them would pray for him off and on all day. He thought about how, at night, his mother would kneel alone beside her bed to pray again. He was silent, embarrassed, until his father asked if anything were wrong.

"After you left us," Stuart said, "did you ever think what you did was a sin?"

His father mashed a black fly that had landed on his wrist. It left a dark smear on his pale skin. "For a long time, that's all I could think of," he said. "But now, I guess I don't think about sin so much any more. There are things people do, and things people don't. People make choices. And some of those choices are hurtful."

Stuart thought about this as his father fitted the first of the posts into one of the holes they had made, and a great feeling of relief washed over him. He thought about his own life, and decided he wanted to try making a choice of his own, without consulting God or his mother or anybody, just to see what would happen. It was then he decided he didn't want to be called *Stuart* anymore; he wanted to be called *Start*. It was still his given name, he'd tell his mother when he got home. After all it was the same word, except for the missing "u." But he knew in his heart it was a very different name, and his mother would sense that immediately. It was a name that meant things like *go* and *begin;* it would carry him places beyond Maine and even Massachusetts, perhaps even as far as the midwest and its open skies and flat, straight roads where there was nothing to trip you up.

"I don't want to get you in trouble with your mother," his father said. "So why don't you just tell her I regret my sins deeply. There, I just said that to you. You don't even have to lie."

Stuart nodded, and his father came over and put his arm around his shoulder. Stuart felt the strength drain out of his legs and ripple away into the ground, and he clung to his father tightly, tightly, and his father hugged him back. A cool breeze lifted his hair, and he sensed that his father expected nothing from him beyond this particular moment. *Think of God as your Heavenly Father,* Pastor Hardy counseled, but with God, there was always a trace of fear, like the faint tang of salt left on your skin after the beach, the possibility that something you had done or were about to do was wrong, and this would be the last straw, the thing that caused God to spew out your soul in disgust. Now, for the first time in Stuart's life, not even in the smallest, meanest part of himself did he feel that he might be found wanting.

"In fall, when the leaves turn, you'll come back and we can go horseback riding," his father said, and he let go of Stuart a bit awkwardly. "There are trails on the state park land up the road. Maybe your mother would even want to come too." Stuart imagined what his mother would have to say about horses, about pastures and black flies and Miriam, about people who thought they wanted to live close to the land like they were animals. It would not be a good idea. He decided not to say anything about changing his name just yet.

The shadows from the Berkshires had covered them completely by the time they started back toward the house. As they came up out of the pasture, Stuart saw that Mars was waiting for them. She was plump like Miriam, and she stood with her feet planted far apart, as if she were daring someone to try and push her off balance. "I know karate," she announced to Stuart. "I can beat you up."

"Oh, sweetheart," his father said wearily. "Can't you say hello like a good girl?"

"No!" Mars shrieked. She grabbed Stuart by his blistered hands and dragged him into the house where she began introducing him to all her stuffed animals. Miriam came in and her eyes met Stuart's, one adult to another, a look that said, *What can I do?*

"It's okay," Stuart said, and he swung Mars up onto his shoulders as she pummeled his neck with karate chops, giggling, hollering, "You're going to die!" When Miriam called to Stuart's father, "Hey, Greg, looks like Mars has finally met her match!" Stuart felt a swift flush of pride. He gripped Mars's bony knees tightly, awed and amazed that there was another person in the world who was made up of some of the same pieces that were contained in his own body. It made him seem larger than he really was. It made him seem capable of more things.

For supper that night, Miriam served tuna casserole, whole milk, creamed corn from a can. In the center of the table was a long loaf of white bread, and a tub of butter stood beside it. Nobody said Grace. Stuart watched as Miriam began to eat that bread, slice after slice, how she buttered it thickly and let her upper lip slide over its glistening surface before easing it into her mouth. He was hungry, not for the bread, but for the obvious pleasure it gave her. She sighed as she ate, long dreamy sighs that even Mars's shrill chatter didn't seem to disturb. At the end of the meal she took another slice, shaped it into a ball and dipped it into the sugar bowl, and he wanted to catch her hand, to pry open her fingers like petals and swallow the gray lump of dough for himself. He had never been to Ohio or anywhere else outside the northeast, but he sensed that this would change. He would call himself Start and grow his hair even longer than his father's. He would fill a backpack with food and walk west until the land became smooth as skin. The earth tones around him would not be something women painted on their bodies, but a part of the moving, breathing land, and they would ring out like a choir. One day, he'd be walking down some flat Ohio road when he'd notice something on the horizon, a house, perhaps, or a flock of drowsy sheep. With that his eyes would be opened, but it would be different from the way Pastor Hardy said. It would be like the feeling he was having now, when you sense you've crossed over to some distant place and stayed just a moment too long, so that returning is no longer a possibility.

Silk

y husband moves his hands over the cat, twirling his fingers in the long, tangled fur behind her ears. She is the third in a series of cats, her name is Chrysanthemum. "Chrissie," he tells her. "Sweet, sweet Chrissie." She squirms deep into the softness of his lap. The television murmurs; a choir is singing Jesus songs, clapping hands, smiling.

"Have you noticed anything," I say, "about David?"

Chrysanthemum is the color of birch leaves in fall. Bill leans to nuzzle his chin into her fur. His dark beard spreads like oil through her chest, and she arches her back, her toes spread wide. "Like a baby," he coos. "Sweet, sweet little baby."

His eyes flick at me; a warning.

I get up and go into our side of the bedroom, which is partitioned off from David's by a faded Indian print. The floor is cold; brown linoleum squares, the same as in the kitchen, the living room, the bath. I am careful not to step on the cracks between the squares. A half-eaten cheeseburger rots on the nightstand, and candy wrappers are scattered everywhere, like dead leaves. Bill is a man who eats constantly. He swallows dirt from the back yard, peanut shells, and laundry detergent. He nibbles the leather trim off my old winter coat, and, at night, he clamps his mouth to my shoulder as he sleeps.

From my pocket I remove a pair of silk panties, extra large, black, with tiny red bows at the hips. I found them this morning, in David's dresser drawer, when I was putting away some shirts he'd left piled on the couch. It was the softness of the panties that startled me; I wove them through my fingers. They were cool, almost damp to the touch. They smelled like gardens, roses, spring.

I've always wanted to own something made of real silk.

Bill lumbers past the bedroom doorway into the kitchen. I tuck the panties back into my pocket and follow him, square by square. He stops in front of the sink and plunges his hands into the gray water. His elbows flex like wings. He brings up a green pan with a broken handle, and fills it with milk and a long squirt of Hershey's. I watch his lips part as the dull arc of chocolate slaps the milk.

David comes up the porch steps and swings into the kitchen, letting the screen door close behind him with a *smack*. Bill's shoulders stiffen. The shape of his bones beneath his T-shirt are like the bones of a very old woman.

"An idle mind is the Devil's workshop," Bill hisses without turning around.

David ignores him. My son's lips are full; cherub's lips. They do not look like the Christ-hungry lips of a child conceived in sin.

"Hey, babe," he says to me.

"Hey," I say.

He goes into the bedroom and disappears behind the Indian print. The bones in Bill's shoulders softly fade away. The panties in my pocket are warm and slick, like a tongue.

2

That night, while Bill is in the bathroom, I step into panties. They're loose in the waist, but the hips fit just fine. I don't put on my night shirt. I arrange myself at the foot of the bed, and when Bill comes out of the bathroom, I grit my teeth in a smile. The gold-plated cross he wears flickers at his throat.

"Uh," he says, a soft, deflated sound. My body is one of Satan's many temptations. Bill's eyes dart around like bees trapped in a jar.

"Mary," he says, "put on something decent." The tips of his ears are flames.

"Guess where I got them."

"Mary."

"Guess."

He shouts, "Take them off!" and hooks a sharp finger into the elastic. I feel a snap; the panties rip. They fly from his hand like a bat. I look at Bill, his fat, hairy shoulders, the color rushing to his forehead and cheeks in patches like clots of blood. My nipples harden into dark and eager bruises. If he gets angry enough, he might have a stroke.

"Mary, goddamnit, cover yourself!"

"Will you two shut up in there?" David calls from behind the Indian print. Bill glares at me, his fists clenched into stones. Then he gets into bed and curls up in a ball, arms around his knees. I turn out the light. Chrysanthemum jumps up on the bed. Bill unfolds, and she spreads like a fan across his chest.

3

Two months ago I found a lavender teddy crumpled in a ball at the back of David's closet. The teddy was no more than a scrap of lace. It hadn't disturbed me much. Fifteen isn't too young to sneak a girl into your room. I took it into the kitchen where David was doing his homework, and told him he was old enough to clean his own goddamned closet from now on. David looked hard at the teddy. Then he shrugged and took it, stuffed it in his pocket.

"You're lucky I didn't show your father."

David said, "It would kill him."

And we laughed at the thought of Bill confronted by a teddy.

"Babe," David said, "can't you imagine it? Can't you just imagine what he'd do?"

David's not afraid of Bill or God or anyone anymore. He is handsome at fifteen. People tell me, *Mary, that child's going to break hearts.* People said that about me, when I was fifteen.

4

Bill starts screaming at one twenty-three. He's on his back, rigid, his legs pumping the pedals of an imaginary bicycle, hurtling over dark hills at a terrifying speed. I snap on the light, record the time; I don't bother trying to wake him anymore. David coughs behind the Indian print and starts to grind his teeth. When he was small, he'd had dreams too, and I was terrified. But they turned out to be nothing. Bill's doctor gave him an EEG and it checked out okay.

Bill's dreams are called *night terrors*. Sometimes he has three in one night. If he'd agree to stay over at the sleep lab, they'd pay him one hundred dollars a month to let a machine record his brain waves. It doesn't matter where he sleeps, he still gets the night terrors. He gets disability for it. During the day, he sits around doing jigsaw puzzles that no one else may touch. He watches religious shows on TV and strokes Chrysanthemum. He tells me that he and I will both be condemned to the lap of the Devil.

I record the exact time and date of all Bill's dreams. Twice a month I call this information over to the lab. They slip me fifty whenever I tell them I'm not going to do it anymore.

5

At breakfast, I stare at David's hair. It's long and rich and shiny looking, as if he takes lots of vitamins. In fact, he lives on Pop-Tarts and Jolly Good Creme Soda and, I suspect, dope with the money that disappears from the pockets of Bill's limp jeans. His catch-all response to everything is *Hey, babe, keep it chilled.*

I've got the torn panties in the pocket of my robe. I snitch a Pop-Tart from his plate, break off half for myself.

"Babe, I left you one in the box."

"This one's toasted," I say. "You going to be around for dinner?"

He shrugs. "Don't know. No. Don't think so."

"How come?" I say. "You got a girlfriend or something? You could bring her over for dinner, if you want."

"Babe, keep it chilled," he says. "I'm just going out with some friends."

"You bring her over, we'll have something special."

David laughs and gets up from the table. He's almost six feet tall, and can rest his elbow on the top of my head like I'm propping him up. He does this now and leans his face down into mine.

"Babe," he says, deadpan. "You know I only have eyes for you."

I say, feeling foolish, "I love you."

"What's the matter, you dying?" he says. "Ma, I love you too."

Bill walks into the kitchen, the belt of his bathrobe trailing behind him like a tail. He gives David a look of unconcealed disgust. He goes to the cupboard and finds a can of Chunky Kitty Stew for Chrysanthemum, who is rubbing her head against his bare calves. Her eyes are wild; electric.

He says to David, "Don't talk filth to your mother."

6

Between David's matresses, I find a pair of gray pantyhose with a line of roses etched down the seams. They are the most beautiful pantyhose I've ever seen. I also find a padded brassiere embroidered with cream-colored lace. In the toe of one of his ice skates I find black fishnet stockings, the old-fashioned kind, they need garters to hold them up. I spend almost an hour looking for the garters; they're curled like snakes in a small canister that used to hold Christmas cookies. I hide everything in the pockets of my bathrobe. My body is the one place Bill never goes snooping around.

Bill is certain I am cheating on him, making plans to leave him. He thinks David's involved somehow, and accuses him of unspeakable things.

I know all about you, Bill tells him. You think you're so smart, but I know.

But Bill doesn't know. I pick up the cookie canister, David's sweet secret. Something that Bill can't touch.

I imagine David in bed at night, waiting for us to fall asleep. Then he gets up, quietly, and eases the bra from between the mattresses. He hooks it awkwardly, hands fumbling behind his back, because he doesn't know that you put a bra on backward first, then hook it, and *then* turn it the right way, hunching your shoulders to slip your arms through the straps. I'd been hoping for a girl until after David was born; then I knew how lucky I was to have a boy. Because a boy doesn't need to be taught such things. A boy comes equipped with what he needs. You feed a boy and clothe him, and hug him if he'll let you, and then stand back and watch as he emerges on his own. You don't worry about anything. You don't worry he'll be raped or killed by a stranger holding a Tootsie Roll. You don't worry that he'll put on fishnet stockings, the kind held up by garters, and parade himself in front of strangers who don't care that he's your son.

No, I think, and I put the cookie canister back. David must have a girlfriend, or several girlfriends, and he keeps these things as mementos, like I used to keep locks of my boyfriends' hair in a diary when I was his age. Bill's had been long and curly, ragged around the ears. I snipped off two inches right in front where it would show, one night after Meeting when the pastor called for sinners and Bill came flying down the aisle like he was yanked there on a string. His soul was shining like a clean, white plate; I saw myself reflected there, and I'd wanted him, then, for my own.

There's not much else I remember about being David's age. I do remember, though, how Bill thought I was beautiful. I married him with David flipping inside me like a fish. I remember how being beautiful, like that, was very, very important.

7

It's early afternoon and David's still at school. Bill sits in the kitchen with Chrysanthemum on his lap. He's got a puzzle spread out on the table, something with sunflowers and kittens and a chubby-cheeked little girl. Two empty potato chip bags are wadded up beside him on the floor. I walk slowly, square by square, until I'm right behind him.

Then I sit down on the only other chair, a metal stool with a padded orange seat. I act like I'm going to pick up one of the puzzle pieces. Bill's eyes fix themselves on my hand.

I ask, "You think I'm beautiful?"

"Don't be stupid," he says.

"I want to know."

"Don't."

"Tell me."

"Don't!"

"Don't," I mimic him and watch, fascinated, as one blue vein struggles to life across his forehead. Another pokes out on his neck. I want to kiss those veins, drag my tongue along their edges. I put my face close to Bill's.

"Do you think I'm beautiful?"

He says, "I think you're shit."

His forehead is smooth as a boy's. I open my mouth to taste it and smell the good wood smoke of the meetinghouse, Bill's shy, dewy hands. His hair had been long enough to pinch into two horses' tails and tie back with the elastic bands I'd taken from my own hair. I'd had him there against the back of the church with the cold moon on our shoulders, his eyes going wide to take it all in, the whites growing whiter, spun with moonlight, the pits of his pupils rigid.

Bill pulls away and slaps my face, jumps to his feet and slaps me again. Chrysanthemum starts to fall, but a claw is hooked into his trouser leg and she cannot work it free. She twists for a moment, squalling, then drops to the floor and shoots behind the stove. I reach for the nearest thing I see and swing it at Bill's mouth, which is open now, dribbling, a coarse and angry sore. I drop the skillet, shaking, and Bill's hands fall to his sides. His eyes bear down on me, shocked into focus; he tests his lip with his tongue. I see myself wavering in his pupils, and I've never been so lovely.

"Jesus, Jesus help us," he weeps. His nose is running like a child's, like it does after he's had a particularly bad dream, when he calls to me

and we cling to each other and he says how much he needs me, *Mary,*
Mary, until my name becomes a song.

I go outside and sit on the stoop. It's a spring day, harsh and bright.
Chrysanthemum pushes her way past the screen, her tail limp and
bewildered. She licks her paw; there's blood around the nail, and I
take her into my lap. I think of how hard it is to live in the world, with
things the way they are and no way to change them, and I think I
understand why David needs his delicate things, lace, lavender, the
softness of real silk.

Silk

Read This and Tell Me What It Says

My father took pills to make him calm, but they never worked the way they were supposed to. Chronically hyperactive, he rubbed his hands on his thighs, banged his knees together, snapped his fingers. He ate with quick, thrusting gulps. He paced as he talked, beginning new sentences in the middle of old ones. He had never learned to read very well because of his short attention span, and it was hard for him to hold a conversation. The doctors said there wasn't anything they could do about it, except give him pills that didn't work.

The pills my brother took were not by prescription. Sullivan would come upstairs from his bedroom in the basement and stare at the walls for hours. He looked so much like my father that sometimes, for a split second, I'd think he was my father *not moving*. He's dead, I'd think, and I'd tease myself with it. I'd think about the way his being dead made me feel.

Once I said to Sullivan, "You know how much you look like Dad?"

He gave me a look that went right through me. He said, "An abysmal misconception; I am nothing like that man." We were listening to the sound of my father riding the stationary bicycle he kept in the laundry room. He biked for at least an hour every day. The chain squeaked with each stroke.

"I didn't say you *were* like him, I said you *looked* like him."

"The man is a goddamn gerbil," Sullivan said. His eyes were my father's; narrow, curving down at the corners, except that the pupils in Sullivan's eyes were huge.

Sullivan was four years older than I was. Being the kid sister got me attention in bad ways as well as good, but I was fifteen and took attention where I could get it. My mother told me again and again how much she had hoped for a daughter, how certain she was when she was carrying me that I would turn out to be exactly what she wanted. I played the piano and sang in the church choir; summers I played volleyball downtown and got a tan. I pretended to read the classics, one by one, as they arrived from the Book of the Month Club, bound in brown vinyl with gold-plated trim. I was becoming, according to my mother, a *well-rounded individual.*

But the thing I liked to do more than anything else was steal. I was really good at it. I was nervous and awkward most of the time, but when I stole I was smooth as cream. My best friend, Suzanne, and I bummed rides to Milwaukee with her older brother. He dropped us off at Grand Avenue, and we moved from shop to shop with our loose-sleeved shirts and our jackets tied around our waists, no make-up, hair tied in ponytails, eyes wide and sweet. The most beautiful thing I ever stole was a hand-blown crystal ball from a jewelry store. It had a tiny blue glass house inside, and if you turned it upside down, snow whirled around. It was nothing like the cheap junk you see at Christmas time; this was for all winter long and the snow looked absolutely real. I gave it to Sullivan as a gift; he cupped it in his hands and stared deep into that blue house for a long time.

"House of cards," he finally said.

"Make sense. Do you like it?"

"Gifts are for the living," he said. "You shouldn't squander your talents on me."

"Give it back, then," I said, but he wouldn't. He glued it to the dashboard of his car.

I didn't know what to make of Sullivan. We had been close when we were younger, and I was always looking for ways to climb back into that closeness. The next week I stole him a hand-tooled alligator-hide wallet, but he just smiled and shook his head, so I gave it to Suzanne. I stole things that I didn't like, things I'd never use. When I stole, my mind grew absolutely still, that stillness you get when you walk into a church and know that you are safe there.

My mother had big plans for me. I was the smart one, the one who would go on to college and make something of myself. My mother was a hair stylist and color consultant; on weekends she trimmed my hair, did my nails, worked on my wardrobe with me, the wardrobe that would impress the friends I made in college. New things were always appearing in my closet, but my mother never asked about them, the same way she never asked why Sullivan, who had graduated from high school a year ago, had so much pocket money and no job.

My mother had not given up on Sullivan. *He's finding himself,* she said. About my dad she said, *He has ants in his pants.* She had phrases that summed up each of us. Mine was, *She will go far.*

She wrote away for information on at least fifty colleges. I was only a sophomore with a C+ average, but at night, we pored over the catalogs together, choosing dorms, sororities, and, occasionally, classes. I was going to major in pre-law or pre-med. I would go to a state university for now, but for graduate school, I'd get a scholarship and hit the Ivy League. When I thought about actually applying for college, I got a strange hot feeling in my head that my mother said was excitement.

My father was proud of the education I was going to get. I liked to read, and if he saw me with a book, he squeezed my shoulder—always too hard—and got Sullivan to do whatever it was he was going to ask me to do. I got out of a lot of work that way. Sullivan mowed the lawn in summer, shoveled snow in winter, painted, did dishes, vacuumed, took out the garbage. My father sometimes picked up my books and asked me to tell him what was in them. He brought me letters, advertisements for things he wanted, recipes.

"Read this," he'd say, "and tell me what it says."

So I'd tell him that Big Charlie and his wife were doing fine, and they hoped to hear from him soon. I'd tell him why Ford meant quality, and how you could hear a pin drop over five hundred miles of phone line if you used SPRINT. When he started to pace, I'd pace behind him, rattling off the facts.

"Good, that's very good," he said, washing his hands in invisible water, shifting from foot to foot, before his mind wandered off to other things. He didn't ask Sullivan to read to him because Sullivan made things up.

Whatever was between Sullivan and my father had started before I was born. When I asked my mother about it, she just rolled her eyes and said, *Boys will be boys,* and gave me a look to let me know I should be satisfied with that answer.

"But what does that mean?" I said.

"Oh," my mother said. "Well. They just have different interests, that's all."

"You mean Dad isn't interested in Sullivan," I said.

"Oh," my mother said, "now, Mary Ann, I don't think that's fair."

My mother kept a picture on her dresser that had been taken on Sullivan's fourth birthday. In it, he sits on my father's lap, looking up at my father's chin which is pointing away from my mother and the camera, Sullivan, the other kids in their party hats. My father's knees are spread wide, the way men sit when their laps are empty, their hands folded across their bellies, and their minds on private thoughts. There is nothing about the way my father sits that would be different if Sullivan wasn't there. Looking at that picture made me feel strange. I wondered how my father had looked when he held me, but all my baby pictures were taken with my mother, and both of us are always smiling.

"Lazy bastard," my father said to Sullivan whenever he saw him on the sofa. "You need to learn what it is to work."

"Show me, big guy," Sullivan said. More than anything else, my father hated to be touched. Sullivan draped his long arms around my father's neck, stood so close that they were hip to hip. My father flapped his hands, chewed his lips.

"Big guy," Sullivan said too sweetly. "You have to learn to relax." Under his breath, he said, "Tight-ass," after my father had gone. He loosened the screws that held the seat of my father's stationary bike in place. He moved all my father's pants to his shirt drawer, and all his shirts to his pants drawer. He thought up dozens of little ways to drive my father crazy. "If the man would only smile," Sullivan once said, but my father was too harried to smile, driven by bursts of energy, unpredictable as lightning bolts, that wiped out whatever was going through his mind and made his hands shake and his jaws bite down hard.

My father worked for UPS and he left in the morning before my mother and I got up. Sullivan didn't open his eyes until noon, so my mother and I ate breakfast at the Donut Hole downtown. The waitresses knew us and automatically brought two coffees and two jelly doughnuts. I dunked my doughnut and squinted out the window, jiggling my foot and thinking about Suzanne and what we would do that day and worrying about it. I worried about everything. My mother was quiet in the morning; she dreaded going to work. Sometimes she talked about playing hooky.

"Let's make a picnic lunch," she'd say. "We can bundle up and eat in the park" or "Let's stay home today and watch TV."

But always, at seven fifty-five, she said, *Another day, another dollar, I guess,* and walked across the street to The Style Haven, and I walked up the hill to school.

Suzanne and I were together all day because we took all the same classes. We called each other every night to discuss the things we forgot to talk about. We did everything together and it drove the teachers wild. Sometimes we'd cut in the afternoon and go to the woods behind the parking lot where Sullivan hung out with his friends. The air drifting from them smelled sweet. Suzanne and I walked over, acting cool, until they'd give us a hit. Being stoned cleared my head and slowed me down. It made me realize how nervous I was all the rest of the time. I was turning into my father and there was nothing I could do about it. I tried a few of my father's pills and they didn't help at all. When I told my mother how I was feeling—that I couldn't keep still, that my palms sweated, that my heart pounded for no reason—she said it was my age and that I should find a boyfriend.

I had a boyfriend. His name was Dirk Smith, and I hadn't told anyone but Suzanne about him because he wasn't the sort of boyfriend a girl admitted to. Dirk had bad breath and pimples the size of dimes. When he kissed me in the bus shelter after all the buses had left, I wanted to spit and wipe my mouth. *This is what normal people do,* I told myself, but it didn't help.

So I got stoned with Sullivan as often as I could and I stole and I ate breakfast with my mother. I read things to my father as he rode the stationary bicycle in the laundry room, shouting to be heard over the squeak of the chain. At night, when my mother pulled out the college catalogs, my heart pounded until I thought it would explode.

Suzanne said not to worry about it. She didn't seem to understand me the way she used to, and this terrified me because if anything happened so we weren't best friends, I didn't know what I'd do.

"You're a victim of stress," she said. "That's normal."

"I guess," I said. "I just feel like I can't shut my brain off. I feel like I'm going crazy."

"It's nerves," Suzanne said, "and you're lucky to have them. Look how skinny you are!"

Suzanne was always on a diet. I was on the track team, the girls' intramural softball team, and I lifted weights in the gym. In the evening, I played the piano for hours to keep my mind from racing around and around what had piled up there during the day. Still, I had insomnia. I had bags like walnuts under my eyes. I was skinnier than anybody else I knew except for one person, and that was my father.

"Sweetheart," he said to me one day. "Read this and tell me what it says."

It was a newspaper article about a man who had an allergy to everything: food, air, people, animals. The man had to live in a special house and wear silk clothes and eat irradiated food. If he didn't, his nerves drove him crazy, he hallucinated, he went without sleep for days. I paced after my father, explaining it to him.

"Maybe that's what's wrong with me," he said.

"Me too," I said eagerly, but his mind had already wandered to other things and he didn't hear. I found a new boyfriend, a short, muscular junior who liked to be called Fonzie, and we spent hours exchanging vicious kisses in the woods behind the parking lot. Fonzie knew what he was doing, but I couldn't keep my mind on it for long. I forgot to finish meals. I asked to use the bathroom during class, and then I sat in the stalls, giggling. I thought, *I am cracking up.*

I knew I would never get into college. When I turned sixteen, my mother gave me a ring that had belonged to her mother. The ring had two diamonds set into a silver band. I couldn't believe she was giving me two diamonds.

"My mom was smart just like you," my mother said. "I always hoped you'd take after her. I think this should belong to you."

"Mom," I said. "I'm not smart like that."

"I was so afraid you'd take after me."

"I am like you."

"No," my mother said, and she made a motion in the air like she was wiping the words away. "You aren't one bit like me."

"That's because there's something wrong," I said. "I can't stop thinking. I can't slow down."

"That's good," my mother said. "You'll never be short of energy."

My mother had a special look she gave me, and that look said I was the smartest, prettiest, most talented girl in the world. It wasn't the sort of look you could argue with. It was a look that had made up its mind. I wore the ring and I passed my driver's ed exam and became addicted to driving *fast*. For the next year, high speed soothed my mind. Even Sullivan wouldn't ride with me.

"There are certain precautions one takes to live a long and fruitful life," he said. I didn't care. I called him chicken-shit and flew around town in my mother's '74 Pinto wagon, running stop signs, squealing curves. Suzanne found a steady boyfriend who drove within the speed limit. He came along with us to Milwaukee, and I thought his face would split, his mouth dropped open that wide, when I slipped a pair of dove-shaped earrings into my jacket. Suzanne wouldn't steal with me after that. She said she had grown up. I tried to give her the earrings, but she told me I should return them.

Read This and Tell Me What It Says

I mourned for Suzanne, especially when I saw her in the halls with girls we had always called *fluff.* I got shin splints and had to quit track, so after school I came home and played the piano and when I'd had enough of that I rode my father's stationary bike. He was pleased we finally had something in common. If he came home before I was finished, he walked circles around me while he waited, talking to himself, gesturing wildly.

"Don't have children," he said to the air. "They'll grow up and stab you in the heart."

I knew he was worried about Sullivan. Sullivan came home less and less, but I saw him every day behind the school. He always was glad to see me.

"Mary Ann," he'd say. "Sweet sister. Flesh of my flesh."

"Hey," I'd say, trying to act cool around his friends who were older and had dropped out or graduated, but Sullivan would muss up my hair, or imitate my walk, or ask how was kindergarten today. His friends didn't know what to make of me. They circled me, just out of reach, like wary dogs. After a while, though, they got used to me, and they became my friends almost as much as Sullivan's. We drove to Milwaukee on weekends and went dancing and partied on the East Side. I was like their mascot. I was everyone's kid sister.

My favorite of Sullivan's friends was a girl named Lace, and at the beginning of my senior year, she and I became best friends. Seeing Suzanne in the halls didn't matter now; Lace and I shared the same *mind.* We cut our hair the same, dated the same guys, and had identical rosebuds tattooed above our ankles. Lace liked to race trains; she took me to where the railroad tracks crossed Highway KW south of town, where three kids had been killed last year, and showed me how it was done. You lined up in however many cars you had, with the bravest kids in the last car. Then you waited for the ten fifty-three freighter. You drank beer, and if another car went past, you all acted like you were leaving so they wouldn't call the cops. When you heard the train in the distance, you got into the cars; at the last possible moment, the first car took off across the tracks with the rest of the cars behind. Sometimes, after the train shuddered past, the last car would still be on the other side of the tracks and you laughed at the kids in it and called them chicken-shit. If everybody made it, you drank more beer to celebrate and told the lead car they were chicken-shit for taking off too soon.

Read
This and
Tell Me
What It
Says

That was how you did it, and Lace and I raced trains every weekend with whoever wanted to come with us. We got reputations as dangerous girls. We wore black lipstick and went on the Pill. We had crying jags together and holed up at Lace's house because her parents were never there. We tried to figure out what I would do after graduation. We tried to figure out what Lace would do when her parents finally threw her out.

Lace liked to hear me play the piano. After school we'd sneak into the practice rooms where I would play Chopin nocturnes and Lace would read Harlequin romances. I had perfect pitch and I played everything by ear. No one had told me this was unusual, so I didn't think about it much. Playing the piano was just something to do that calmed me down for a while. The music teacher, Mr. Lee, took an interest in me. I told him I liked romantic music, so he brought in a recording of the Chopin *Berceuse.* I thought I would die listening to it, and afterward I went to the piano and played what I remembered of it.

"You could be famous," Lace said.

"Nobody gets famous playing the piano," Mr. Lee said, "but you have a gift, a remarkable gift." He wanted to make an audition tape of me and send it to a conservatory out east. I shrugged at him.

"Whatever," I said.

"You have to get moving on this," he said. "Application deadlines are in January. Unless," he said, "you have an interest in another field?"

It was December and I had no interest in anything. One day after school, he tape-recorded me playing the Chopin Ballads. All I knew was romantic music, and almost all of it was Chopin. Mr. Lee said not to worry. He said if anyone complained, he'd swear we'd made a classical tape and a contemporary tape and they must have been lost in the mail. Then he took me out for dinner.

"To celebrate," he said. We drove to Sheboygan because he said he knew a restaurant there that served fantastic steaks. The restaurant was called Pancake Heaven, and it served breakfast All Day Every Day. It was attached to a motel. Mr. Lee ordered a rare steak with his eggs and talked about evolution.

"Man evolved as a carnivore," he said. "I never understood folks who try to undo that particular process."

He smiled as I bit into a piece of bacon.

"This is what separates us from apes," he said. He reached for my hand and squeezed it between his fingers. "You're a talented girl, Mary Ann."

I squeezed his hand back to see what he would do; he blushed the color of his steak, then he pulled my hand to his mouth.

"I've had my eye on you," he said.

"Mr. Lee," I said. "I don't think I want to major in music. I mean, I think my mother wants me to be a doctor."

"Don't limit yourself," Mr. Lee said. He pressed my hand to his cheek; I tugged it free and put both my hands on my lap. "Keep all your avenues open."

I thought about sleeping with Mr. Lee. I looked at his hair cut too short on the top and the eyelash clinging to his cheek. His teeth crossed slightly in front; the crevice between was stained the color of dirt. I decided I couldn't do it, even if it would be an interesting experience to look back on.

"I don't think so," I said.

His hands found mine under the table. "Come on," he said. "I'll fill out the forms. I'll even pay your application fees, how's that for reasonable?"

"Suit yourself," I said.

"That's what attracted me to you in the first place," Mr. Lee said. "You're so mature for your age. Now, I'm going to pay this bill, and then we can either get back in the car and I'll take you home, or," he stroked my hands, "we can go next door. It's your decision."

He smiled, but his eyes were hard as stones.

"I'll wait in the car," I said, and he didn't speak to me all the way back. I felt weird about the whole thing and avoided the practice rooms after that. Lace came over after school the next day and I played the piano in the living room while she leafed through my father's current *Playboy*. I played the *Bercuese*, changing it here and there so that it wouldn't belong to Mr. Lee anymore, but to Lace and myself.

"I'd never look like this," she said when I finally got up to fix coffee. She was studying Miss December. "Not even with plastic surgery."

"Yes, you would," I said. Modeling was the only thing Lace thought she might be good at. She looked like a model, with high cheek bones and long blonde hair that was more white than yellow, but whenever I made an appointment for her with one of Sullivan's photographer friends, she said she was too fat to shoot a portfolio yet. "They air brush everything," I said. "No one has skin like that."

"She does," Lace said. "It's for real, you can tell."

"Lace."

"I think I'm going crazy," Lace said. "I don't know what I'm going to do. I think I am truly insane."

"I think I am too," I said.

"Then what's the point," Lace said, "if we're going to be crazy like this all our lives?"

My mother filled out ten applications for ten different schools and signed my name. She did the writing because her penmanship was nicer; I sat across from her and answered questions.

"How should we write your name?" she said. "Mary A. Crill? M. A. Crill?"

"What's wrong with Mary Ann?"

"Well," my mother looked embarrassed. "Your father picked it out, and it's a very nice name and all, but it doesn't have . . . "

"Flair," I said.

"Exactly. We need something bold, but not pushy."

"How about Marianne, all in one word?"

"Marianne Crill, Marianne Crill," my mother said. "I like the sound of that."

"Me too," I said, and she watched as I practiced signing my new name. My average had slipped to a C– but I told her I'd raised it to a high B. When the school called to report I'd been missing from certain classes, I said I was having menstrual cramps or that I'd come in late or that the teacher just hadn't seen me. I kept finding notes from Mr. Lee in my locker. *Thinking of you*, the notes said. The writing was cramped and jumbled together. *Want to talk. Misunderstanding.*

"What am I going to do?" I asked Sullivan.

We were lying side by side on his waterbed in the basement, listening to Pink Floyd on his two-thousand-dollar stereo system. A large tank of tropical fish was suspended by thin chains from the ceiling, and the underwater lights inside the tank were the only lights in the room. The fish glowed electric orange, blue, the bright colors of dragonflies, and in the darkness they seemed to float on air.

"Relax," Sullivan said. "We shall move to Milwaukee. We shall live in harmony with our fellow creatures. Milwaukee will broaden our horizons."

I had three hundred dollars in savings from various jobs that I quit within weeks of taking them. "We don't have the money to move anywhere," I said. "Besides, it would look weird."

"Money is not a relevant issue. Trust," he said, "is key." He rested his head against my shoulder. "We can make a break from things here. This summer I'm going to get clean."

"Why this summer?" I said. "Why not now?"

"The world of high finance can be troublesome," Sullivan said. "One acquires certain responsibilities."

I had no responsibilities. I lived for racing trains. One night, Lace and I went to the tracks alone. It was a cold night in March; there were no stars, and the faint glow of the town in the distance made me shiver. We were drinking Southern Comfort. We walked to the tracks, passing the bottle back and forth, and sat back to back between the rails.

"You're the best friend I've ever had," she said.

"You too."

"No, I mean that."

"Me too," I said. We felt the rails start to hum and watched the wide, pure eye of the train grow wider; Lace's pale hair exploded with light.

"Let's go," I said.

"Not yet."

"Now," I said. I had to yell to be heard. I got up and grabbed her hands, but she tucked them under her arms. The bottle tipped against the tracks. I jumped back onto the road and as the train roared up Lace unfolded her arms and sailed into my chest. The impact knocked me down; the back of my head hit the ground hard as the Southern Comfort bottle spun through the air above us. Lace rolled off me, laughing.

"Chicken-shit," she said.

64

"Asshole," I said, surprised at myself. I had never been angry with Lace before; her eyes opened wide with hurt. I hugged her, then, and she hugged me back and we stood there hugging until I felt foolish and pulled away.

"I'm sorry," I said. "I'm just drunk."

My mother was waiting up when I got home. Three more universities had rejected me. That made ten. "It's not fair," she said. "After we worked so hard."

"Oh, Mom, don't," I said, but her face flushed and she started to cry.

"Oh, Mary Ann," she said, only she said it *Marianne.*

"I'm just not that smart," I said. I could smell Lace's perfume on the collar of my coat and it distracted me. I spoke very slowly and carefully, trying hard not to seem like I'd been drinking. "I've been telling you that all along."

"But you are," my mother said. She blew her nose. "We'll figure something out," she said. I could tell by the way she looked at me she didn't blame me one bit. My stomach clenched. I went to bed, but later I got up and vomited Southern Comfort.

Lace took all of her mother's Valium and walked out into the snow. The cops found her in the woods south of town, not far from the tracks. They said she looked like she was sleeping, but her parents cremated the body right away and so I never saw. Cops and reporters asked me questions because I was The Best Friend. I said she hadn't seemed depressed. I said she wasn't any different from the rest of us.

After that, I stayed home from school for days. My mother told my teachers I was grieving, but all I did was pull the stationary bicycle into the living room so I could bike and watch TV at the same time. I couldn't sleep. I couldn't make decisions. I didn't know what I was going to do next.

"Leave things to me," Sullivan said. "You've had a terrible shock." He started looking for a two-bedroom for us on the south side of Milwaukee. I wasn't convinced I wanted to move away with Sullivan, but on Easter morning, I found a brightly colored straw basket hanging from my bedroom door. It was filled with chocolate eggs and marshmallow rabbits. The card said, *We will get a fresh start. We will live our lives. You'll see.* I loved him so much then I went back into my room and cried and decided to go with him.

I went to Mass with my parents as I always did Easter Sunday. Afterward, my father had my mother read him all of my university rejections. By the time she finished, his face was slick with sweat. I was sitting at the table, listening, and he came over and put his hand on my shoulder. He squeezed so hard I gasped, but though his mouth worked, no words came. Then he patted my hand and went into the laundry room. The chain on the stationary bike began to squeal.

"He feels so bad for you," my mother said.

The next day, when I came home for supper, my father handed me a letter from the Eastman School of Music.

Read This and Tell Me What It Says

"Read this and tell me what it says," he said, but the letter had been opened and I saw by his face that he already knew. My mother was smiling so hard that she didn't look like herself. I read that I had been accepted at the conservatory, based on my fine audition tape. I would be placed on academic probation for a year. I was to be congratulated.

My father jumped up and down. My mother said she hadn't applied for me at Eastman, and I told her one of my teachers at school had done it for me.

"We wanted to surprise you," I said numbly, and she hugged me and my father pounded me on the back.

"Where's Sullivan?" I said. His Camero was parked outside on the street, but of course, no one knew where he was. That night in my room, I got down on my knees and tried to send psychic messages, first to Lace, then to Sullivan. With Lace, I felt a warm tingle in my stomach, and I knew she was happy for me. But with Sullivan I felt nothing, though I tried to reach him for a long time. I knew if he still wanted me to move to Milwaukee, that was where I would go. *Sullivan,* I whispered hard inside my head. Through the door, I could hear my mother on the phone, the shrill rise and fall of her voice, as she called her sisters, her old school friends, telling them our good news. I covered my ears and repeated Sullivan's name until it became just a sound.

The following night, when we heard he'd been arrested, I drove Sullivan's Camero down to the railroad tracks and crossed just seconds before a train pounded through. It came so close to hitting me that the force of the air swung the tail end of the Camero out to the side. I pulled over and got out. The sky was speckled with stars; I threw back my head and breathed deeply. For the first time in many weeks, my head was clear. I was filled with what I'd felt as I crossed the tracks, just after that moment when I knew I wouldn't make it: the unexpected relief that I'd been wrong.

Read This and Tell Me What It Says

Lies

I slept in the same bed with my cousin Nancy until I was ten years old. After that my aunt said I was grown up and she bought me my own bed, a used metal cot that someone had painted white with pink flowers. She put the cot next to Nancy's bed and at night we held hands across the open space between us. Nancy was eleven and wore rings on all her fingers; I traced each one until I knew them by heart.

Our room was the attic, and when it was too hot to sleep, we lay naked on top of the sheets and talked about whether we were good looking. I had dishwater hair and crooked teeth, but we would pretend I had long blonde hair and straight white teeth and breasts like Nancy. Nancy looked just like my aunt; I didn't look like anyone at all. My aunt said I probably looked like my father, who none of us had ever seen.

Nancy liked to tell lies. When people asked where my father was, she told them he died of an allergy to bananas or that he collected octopus eggs off the coast of France. She told people I was quiet because I was a genius, and that I had invented the first household anti-gravitational device when I was eight years old. She told them I had been bitten by two different kinds of poisonous snakes and lived. She tried to teach me to lie, but I couldn't learn no matter how hard we practiced. Some boy in the park who really liked Nancy would say to me, Hey, what's your name? I could feel Nancy give me a look, but I always said Jane, which was my real name, instead of Londa or Beulah Lee or Sparky the way Nancy would have done. When a boy asked Nancy for her phone number, she gave them the number to the police station. When a boy asked Nancy how old she was, Nancy told them fifteen.

You have to be real dumb to believe a lie, Nancy said.

My aunt didn't know what to do about Nancy. Nancy, she said, was out of control. When Nancy would put on her white summer skirt with the lacy blouse that scooped at the neck, my aunt put her head in her hands. You know what you look like? my aunt would say.

Nancy had a secret boyfriend. His name was Edward Martin, and he was thirty-six years old. We knew because Nancy had stolen his wallet from where he'd left it on the front seat of one of his cars. We spied on him from behind the lilacs as he worked in his back yard, taking pieces of his cars apart, taking apart those pieces. Edward Martin wore cut-off shorts and shirts hanging from his waist by their sleeves. He drank beer and tapped the ashes from his cigarettes into the empty cans. Nancy stole one of the cans and smudged the ashes on our foreheads. This will make us invisible to him, she said, but she was wrong.

One day when we turned around he was behind us and his arms were full of lilacs. How come you two watch me all the time? he said, and when we didn't answer he said, Do you like cars? He split the lilacs into two bunches. Here, you can have these, he said, and gave one to each of us.

We like cars, Nancy said, and she tossed her hair. I like cars particularly. I'm going to buy one for myself next year when I turn sixteen.

We followed him into his yard and he walked from car to car, explaining what was wrong with each one and what he was doing to fix it. We scratched the backs of our legs. We chewed the tips of our braids. You're not interested in cars, he said, well how 'bout kitty-cats? You girls like kitty-cats? He pointed to an old yellow Cadillac that was missing one of its doors. You take a look in there, he said, and on the floor half under the front seat was a mama cat with her babies.

Can I hold one? I said, but the mama cat hissed and her teeth were long and thin and white. Her pupils filled her eyes until they were solid black. She didn't look like any kind of cat I had ever seen.

69

She tried to bite you! Nancy said.

But you know why she does that? Edward Martin said. When we didn't answer, he said, You know how things get born? She went through all of that and that's why now she protects them. They are all she cares about. You'll be the same way when you have babies, he said, and he was looking hard at Nancy.

That's a lie, Nancy said. I would never be that way.

Yes, you will, Edward Martin said. You'll grow up and have a baby and you'll be just the same.

No I won't, Nancy said. You're not me so how can you say what I'm going to be like?

Her voice was high and squeaky and she did not sound fifteen. She dropped the lilacs on the grass and walked away with her braid bouncing hard between her shoulders like it did when she was mad. Nancy, you going home? I yelled, but she wouldn't answer. I didn't want to have to look at Edward Martin, so I looked at the mama cat again and the kittens tucked tight to her belly.

Do you want a baby someday? he asked, and I said, yes, I did.

You're so sweet, still, you little ones, he said, and he ran his hand over my hair. He said I could pick out names for the kittens. I named them Nancy, all six of them.

Evolution of Dreams,
North of Sheboygan, 1986

Pip had been out of work for seven months. His older sister, Elaine, gave him weekly ultimatums. *If you don't have a job by Friday, you're out. If you don't get an interview by Tuesday, that's it.* It was not that Elaine was uncaring; she was under serious pressure from her boyfriend, Ajax, who owned the trailer they all were living in and who was noticing that the longer he knew Pip, the less he liked Elaine.

Pip was nineteen, with large, doughy hands and feet, and a face that was furrowed with acne. Pale hairs sprouted from the rims of his ears. He wore faded T-shirts with sayings on them like *SHIT HAPPENS* and *VIRGINITY CAN BE CURED,* and his stomach peeked out beneath those shirts like a lewd and fleshy smile.

"You got to put your best foot forward," Elaine told him between brisk bites of her English muffin. Ajax was sleeping in: he worked second shift as an orderly at the Trauma Center downtown.

"You got to make them think you're this great deal, see, and they better snap you up quick."

Pip was on his fourth bowl of cereal. He dwarfed the tiny breakfast nook, and his feet, which were splayed to avoid the table legs, smelled like something that didn't belong indoors. He shook the cereal box, then dug through it with his fingers, trying to find the prize.

"You need to look 'em straight in the eye."

"Wow, I got it," he said, and he held out a blue plastic ring.

Elaine sighed. She was only ten pounds lighter than Pip, with the same sandy hair and pale complexion. Her hair was cropped close except for one wild tuft which she dyed orange and let fall across her forehead, and there was a bruise high on her cheek that her make-up did not quite conceal.

"Great," she said. "Could you be serious for just one minute here?"

"Okay," said Pip, and he dropped the ring in the trash.

"Okay," said Elaine. "You got any leads on a job?"

"Not really, but I was thinking," Pip said. "There's a class on cake decorating at the Y."

"Pip."

"No, what I mean is, I could maybe work at a bakery, if I knew how to decorate cakes."

"Nobody is going to hire you because you took a ten-dollar class at the Y! Damnit, Pip." She looked at her watch, then got up and grabbed her coat which was hanging over a hook on the wall. Her fingernails were almost an inch long, and she was careful of them as she poked her arms through the sleeves.

She said, "Ajax wants one hundred dollars from you by next Friday. Today is Tuesday. If you get something today, you can do it. Go to Burger King or McDonalds. Go anywhere, just apply for something, okay?"

Pip didn't think he would like working at a Burger King. He filled his bowl with more cereal.

"Jesus Christ, save some of that! We're on a *budget* here." Elaine buttoned up her coat. "And try to be out when Ajax gets up," she said. "I got to go."

Elaine had once dreamed of becoming a fashion designer; now she worked as a hair stylist at the mall just south of town. There was always work for a stylist; she secretly hoped that Pip would become a stylist too. She'd even phoned his name and address to the Community Stylist Academy, but Pip still hadn't read the information they'd sent.

"I got to go," she said again. She opened her purse and patted powder on her bruise, using the window in the door for a mirror.

Then she snapped the purse closed, lifted her chin, and set out for the bus stop.

"Have a nice day," Pip called after her. He meant it. He loved Elaine more than anyone else in the world. As a child, she marched him back to his bedroom whenever his socks didn't match. She fixed his breakfast every day and scrubbed his face with a clean wash cloth. At night she worked his fractions for him. That was back in Sheboygan, the year their mother disappeared. Their father lived in another state with his girlfriend and their baby, and Elaine didn't feel they should bother him about it. She and Pip lived alone for seven months, budgeting the cash he sent when he remembered. Eventually, their mother came home with a man named Jones.

"This is my new husband," she said, as if she'd never been away. "He's going to be like a father to you."

Elaine hadn't even blinked. "Wipe your feet," she told them, and they did.

Pip ate another bowl of cereal and finished off the rest of the English muffins. He made a pot of coffee and scrubbed a clean patch on the breakfast nook table, where he laid a crisp white piece of paper and a pen that said *GO PACKERS* down the side.

The local newspaper had a lonely hearts column that ran opposite the job listings, and Pip had decided to take out an ad. The only girlfriend he'd ever had was when he was in high school. She hadn't been too much of a girlfriend. Her name was Blossom and she lived each summer in a cardboard box by the railroad tracks. In winter she went away. She never wrote. Pip was impressed by her muscular arms and the heart-shaped tattoo just left of her chin. Sex between them was infrequent, because Pip felt he was too young for all that, and Blossom, that she was too old.

Lately he thought about Blossom whenever he saw Ajax rest his small, furry hand on the back of Elaine's neck. Thinking about Blossom made him lonely and anxious. At night he couldn't sleep, and his stomach hurt during the day. He thought another relationship might help to calm him down.

Young male, he wrote, and then he scratched out *young.* Then he put it back in again, just in case it mattered to somebody, but then he scratched it out again because he figured it was nobody's business, *wants female eighteen to forty-five to be friends with and possible romance, who has a dog.* Pip missed his dog, Donald, who still lived with his mother and Jones in Sheboygan, forty miles away. Donald was a strapping yellow mongrel with arthritic hips. Elaine despised him. After thinking for a while, Pip finally added, *Please make my dreams come true.*

He counted the words up carefully; under thirty, which was two dollars and fifty cents. The coffee was ready, and he got up and poured himself a cup just as Ajax started to curse. Ajax cursed every day when he woke up; long, bubbling streams of curses. Ajax was bitter and depressed. He hated his job at the Trauma Center, the smug, trim nurses and vain doctors, although he realized, too, that it was the best job he could ever hope to get. Sometimes late at night, when tiredness made him calm, Ajax would cry into Elaine's wide lap. Pip couldn't help but hear those shy, breathless sobs that seeped like dampness through the thin walls of the trailer, but he misunderstood what they were about, and thought wistfully of Blossom's wide green eyes.

Pip abandoned his coffee; he folded his ad and slipped it into his pocket. He listened until he thought he heard Ajax's curses winding down. Then he walked to the end of the narrow hallway and scratched on the master bedroom door.

"Goddamnit to hell," said Ajax.

"I need to borrow two dollars and fifty cents," said Pip. "Is that okay?"

"You piece of shit. You dog-faced piece of shit." He sounded muffled.

"Can I come in?"

Pip pushed through the door. Ajax lay face down on the bed with his head jammed deep beneath the pillows. His back was a matted wall of hair.

"Goddamn, *goddamn* son of a bitch."

Pip found Ajax's wallet, which was on top of the dresser, and took out three limp bills. "I'm taking three dollars," he said. "I'll bring back the fifty cents."

"Jesus H. Christ," said Ajax.

Pip put on his coat and walked downtown, where he placed the ad at the newspaper. He realized then he'd forgotten his own copy, the one with Elaine's neat red circles and x's and stars indicating where he should look for jobs and in what order. And he didn't feel right buying another paper with the fifty cents he had left over from the ad, because he had promised Ajax the change.

Instead, he walked around the downtown, thinking about Donald, and staring into shop windows until people came out to ask if they could show him something. He paused by a phone booth, and imagined calling his mother. He tried to think about what he would say. But his mother had wanted him out of the house almost as much as Jones, so there was no point in calling home.

Jones had disliked Pip from the start and promptly set out to change him. He called him by his real name, *Peter,* which sounded forced and strange. He made him watch wrestling on Saturday nights and drink beer and take puffs off his cigars, to toughen his guts. Pip knew his guts were hopelessly frail. He thought the wrestlers were ugly, and one night he said that to Jones.

"What are you, some kind of fairy?" Jones said, and he knocked Pip across the room. From that point on, Jones drank alone. Pip was relieved. The beer had made him queasy. He hid under his bed with Donald, stroking the dog's broad, smooth forehead and talking to him about dreams which would someday make them both famous. For Pip was going to be an astronaut. He'd discover a new planet, a big, beautiful planet, where people could go if they were tired or sick and wanted to be happy. The planet would be named *Donald's Hill* after a small rise south of Sheboygan where Pip took Donald for his slow, painful walks each spring.

At lunch time, Pip stopped at the soup kitchen where he ate a bowl of tomato soup and a bread-and-butter sandwich with Stacy. Stacy had been looking for a full-time job for over a year. Weekends, he worked for three fifty an hour as custodian at the grade school, and during the week he looked for a position in his field, which was hotel management. He'd met Pip at the state employment center, where Pip had been looking specifically for a job that involved exotic animals.

"Pip!" said Stacy. "My good buddy."

"I have been thinking," said Pip, sitting down and reaching across the long metal table for the salt. "I think I would like to decorate cakes."

"Well, that's good, I guess," said Stacy. "It's important to set a job objective. That's what they tell you, anyhow."

"And this morning I put an ad in the paper for a girlfriend."

"Did you put something in about mowing lawns?"

"What?"

"That's what you do, with spring around the corner. You advertise for lawn work. You can make five an hour, and folks'll hire you regular for the summer if they like you."

Pip shook his head. "I just want a girlfriend."

"Don't we all," said Stacy. "But isn't your sister going to throw you out?"

"It's not my sister," said Pip. "It's Ajax."

"Oh, Ajax," said Stacy.

"Ajax is under a lot of stress."

Stacy looked at Pip as though he'd dropped off the moon. "Christ, man, what are you going to do? I can get you something at the school, maybe. Night work, minimum wage, but it's better than nothing."

Pip wiped his mouth with the back of his hand and stood up. "No thank you," he said. "I have a few more things I'd like to try."

In fact, Pip had been thinking about the mouse situation back at the trailer. It was getting out of hand. There were too many mice and not enough crumbs, and lately they were chewing the cords to various kitchen appliances and electrocuting themselves. Elaine had set traps behind the stove, and during the night Pip winced at the short, sharp *smacks.* What if he caught the mice, and tamed them, and built cages for them and sold them as pets? He would be his own boss, then, and Ajax respected a man who was his own boss. For the rest of the afternoon, Pip walked around the downtown and thought about ways to catch mice.

That night, Elaine was furious because she'd found the newspaper with the neat red circles and x's on the counter, exactly where she'd left it. Pip tried to explain about the mice, but Elaine wasn't in a listening mood: it was Ajax's night off, and they were going drinking at Tiny Joe's.

"You see?" Ajax said to Elaine. "He's just a lazy son of a bitch. He's taking you and me for all he can."

Pip felt bad. After they left, he decided to buy Elaine her own trailer. It would be blue, with four bedrooms, instead of just two, and there would be blue velvet curtains in the living room and a big-screen TV. Thinking about this made him feel better, and he thought about it until it was too late to build mouse cages and time to go to bed.

In the morning he got up late. Elaine was already gone, but the paper with his printed personal was waiting on the table. To celebrate, Pip opened a new jar of peanut butter and ate half of it with his finger; the rest he smeared around the base of the stove. Then he sat on the kitchen floor, waiting for a mouse to appear. He kept a large plastic bowl beside him, which he planned to drop over the mouse. While he waited, he read and re-read his personal. He thought it was written with a special flair. He wondered about the women who would call, and he pictured them different ways: some older, mysterious; some young, with large breasts and perspiring hands; some that spoke no

English whatsoever but stared at him in a way that let him know he was understood. To all of them he said the same thing. *You have made my dreams come true.*

When he heard Ajax wake up and start to curse, Pip went out and wandered around town. Midmorning, he stopped at the library for a nap. At lunch time, he hung around the soup kitchen and listened politely as Stacy told him how wild mice could not be tamed and how Pip should come with him to the grade school to see about being a janitor.

The next morning, he caught his first mouse. It literally walked into his lap, startling him out of his daydreams, and he picked it up by the tail. The mouse arched its back and kicked its feet, and it gave Pip a wide-eyed indignant sort of look. It shit three little turds which fell to the kitchen floor.

Pip dropped it into the big plastic bowl, but the mouse promptly climbed back up the sides. Pip admired its spunk. He caught it by the tail again and held it that way while he thought. Then he filled the bowl with an inch of water and put the mouse back in. The mouse bobbed and paddled, but couldn't climb, so it rested with its front paws braced against the sides.

"Shit!" bellowed Ajax from the bedroom.

Pip turned away to get more peanut butter from the refrigerator. He figured that the best way to tame the mouse was to feed it so that it would know he was a friend. Ajax stumbled out of the bedroom in his boxer shorts, and came down the narrow hallway to the kitchen, thumping the walls with his fists. His eyes were swollen and red.

"Scum-sucking pig," he said to Pip. He looked into the bowl. "Jesus Christ," he said. "What the hell!"

"I'm going to sell him," Pip said proudly. "I'm starting my own business."

Ajax spat, "You sell mice?"

"Yes."

"How much?"

"Five bucks, I think."

"You *think*," said Ajax. He scratched his belly violently, raking his fingers through the dark hair. Then he rubbed his eyes and went back down the hallway to the master bedroom. A minute later, he was back, holding a five-dollar bill.

"Five bucks buys me a mouse," said Ajax. "Five bucks for a fucking mouse from my fucking kitchen."

"Yes."

Ajax threw the five on the table. Then he grabbed the mouse by the tail and swung it hard against the counter. Mouse juices splattered across the floor and into the sink; the mouse jerked once and was still.

Pip left the house without his coat or the five-dollar bill. He knew it was cold, but he didn't feel anything. He walked downtown to the newspaper to find out if anyone had answered his personal. The receptionist gave him a small, sad smile. Then she handed him a note card neatly printed with a name and a phone number.

He used the pay phone on the corner across the street. His hands were blue and stiff, and he dropped the quarter twice. It was one of the quarters he'd forgotten to give back to Ajax two days ago.

"Hello," he said "I want to speak with Claire?"

"You got her."

"I'm Pip," he said. "I'm the ad in the paper."

"Oh," she said. "That was fast."

"Yes," said Pip. "Thank you for making my dreams come true."

There was a long pause. "How queer is this going to be?" she finally said. "I mean, what's all this about a dog?"

"My sister doesn't like dogs, so if you have a dog, I thought maybe you could bring it? I mean, if we have a date? I mean, I really miss Donald."

Claire did not say anything.

"Donald is my dog. He lives with my mother in Sheboygan."

Pip waited.

"I'm having a real bad day," he finally said.

"How old are you?" said Claire.

"Nineteen." Pip clamped the receiver beneath his chin, and tucked his hands under his armpits to warm them.

"I'll meet you tonight at the park," Claire said.

"Thank you," Pip said. His eyes were tearing, and his voice was hoarse and strange.

"Six thirty," she said. "My dog's name is Star."

Pip went straight to his room when he got home and crawled into his cot, burrowing beneath the blankets to get warm. He heard Ajax come in, and then Elaine. He listened to them argue for a while, and then he got out of bed and put on all his clothes, layer after layer. He hummed to himself, a low tuneless buzzing.

"You said Friday!" Elaine screamed. "He has nowhere else to go!" Ajax said something back. There was a crash, and then a few more crashes.

When Pip walked into the kitchen, his arms stuck stiffly out from his sides because of all the clothes he was wearing. The air smelled of peanut butter. Elaine was on the floor by the refrigerator; blood spilled from her nose, and three of her nails were broken. Ajax was breathing heavily through his mouth.

"I just wanted to tell you," Pip said, "I got a job."

"Oh!" said Elaine. She struggled to her feet and steadied herself against the wall.

"I have to relocate. To Nebraska. I have to leave tonight."

Ajax pushed past Pip, and stalked down the hall to his room. He shouted, "Nebraska has to be better than this goddamn hell hole!"

"Oh, Pippy," said Elaine.

Ajax slammed the bedroom door.

"It's in sales," said Pip. "It won't pay much at first, but I can get promoted. It doesn't take long to get promoted, only three days."

"You don't have a job," Elaine said.

"I'll be selling vacuum cleaners. And refrigerators."

She started to cry.

"And automobiles," Pip said. "So I can send you money soon. I'm going to buy you a trailer."

Elaine wiped her nose with the back of her hand. Her hand came away bright with blood. She looked at the blood and then up at Pip as though she didn't know what blood was and was waiting to be told.

Pip walked outside and headed toward the downtown. He walked quickly, because it was six o'clock, and he didn't want to be late for Claire. In the park, he sat on a bench and tried not to think about how hungry he was. A girl walked past, munching on an apple, and she tossed it, half-eaten, into a trash can chained to the side of a tree. Pip waited until she was out of sight, and then he went over to the tree and dug through the trash for the core. There was plenty of fruit left on it; it tasted cold and sweet. He found other things too: sandwich crusts, half a banana, the butt end of a hot dog. His hunger rose and choked him; he gasped, sat down hard on the ground, and tried to put everything into his mouth at one time.

"My God," someone said. "You're not Pip, are you?"

Pip turned and saw a woman in a shabby fur coat. She had a small dog wrapped up in her arms. Her cheeks were heavily rouged, and her lips looked chapped and puffy. She wore no gloves; there was dirt beneath her nails.

"Are you Pip?" she said.

He nodded.

"I'm Claire," she said. Her ears were red with cold. "I don't think this will work. I mean, I usually date businessmen, or, you know, people who can pay. This is what I *do*," she said. "Do you understand?"

She didn't look at Pip; instead she spoke to the dog, which raised its head and lifted its fragile ears.

"Is that your dog?" Pip said dumbly. There was banana around his mouth.

Claire nodded. "Star."

"Can I hold him? Just for a minute?"

She looked uncertain.

"My dog has arthritis," Pip said. "In his hips. If you try to pick him up, he cries."

Claire bit her lip. There was a dark sore at the corner of her mouth. "Star is a her, not a him," she said. Then she squatted and opened her arms.

Pip held out his hand, and Star tiptoed toward him. Her body shook with the cold.

"That's a girl," he said. "Come on, sweet girl."

She put a delicate paw on Pip's knee, and he stroked her and buried his face in her fur. He did not move until he felt Claire's hand, rough and sweet, on his shoulder.

"You okay?" she said. "Y'know, Star likes you. She usually don't like strangers, neither."

"You mean it?" said Pip. "You think so?"

Claire smiled a little. "You really are just a child," she said. "I can't have nothing to do with a child."

"I wish I could go home," Pip said.

Star reared up her hind legs, then, and licked at the banana on his face. Her tongue was rough and wet as a washcloth. Pip gratefully bent his head. No matter what would happen, and no matter what would not, for this one moment it all was right, as Star's bright tongue moved over him.

osie hugs her bigger baby sideways on her hip and hollers down the hallway for Wally to hurry up. The baby kicks, and Meryl can hear the crackle of its diaper. Rosie sticks her long middle finger down into the diaper to see if it's wet. It's dry.

"You'd be amazed how much they pee," Rosie says. She wears a pair of tight jeans held together at the top of the zipper by a safety pin. Her breasts have stained two small, wet circles on the front of her shirt.

Meryl gives Rosie a bored look. "I know."

"Maybe you *think* you know," Rosie says. She rocks her wide hips from side to side and raises her chin like a bird. Her littler baby wheezes in the wash basket by the sink. This baby is so little it still doesn't have a name. It's a Down syndrome baby, and its long, pinched eyes make it look wise, although Meryl's parents say it won't ever have much sense. Meryl's parents live along the lake front in a house with five bathrooms, including a private one for Meryl, and an oval swimming pool.

Poor Rosie, Meryl's mother says. Meryl's mother and Rosie's mother are sisters. When they speak to each other their voices are careful, reedy, their smiles held too tight.

Rosie shifts the bigger baby toward Meryl, and Meryl reluctantly takes it. She is sleek in designer jeans and a soft silk sweater that hugs her thin chest and shoulders. The baby's fingers twist into the sweater, and its eyes open wide. A bubble of spit expands between its lips.

"The emergency numbers are by the phone. If you have any problems, just call us at The Gander."

Meryl says, "Jesus Christ, Rosie, I'm seventeen, I *think* I know how to baby-sit. Jesus!" She takes one of Rosie's cigarettes off the table, lights it, awkward with the baby. The baby tucks into her neck like a tick.

"You think you know a lot," Rosie snaps, and then Wally comes into the kitchen so she drops her chin and doesn't say anything else. An angry voice pokes Wally's own anger which seems to live deep in his full, soft belly, an anger that can linger for weeks in the air like smoke.

Rosie had to marry Wally. They'd had a big wedding at St. Michael's with six bridesmaids, dozens of roses, and a wine and cheese reception afterward in the basement.

"My daughter might have made a mistake," Rosie's mother said to Meryl's mother during the ceremony, "but she *is* getting married in the Church."

Meryl's mother didn't marry in the Church; she married a divorced man, an atheist, who owns a successful company. This makes Meryl an infidel. Rosie's mother says that Meryl's mother traded her faith for cash. Meryl's mother says that Rosie's shotgun wedding set her family back financially at least five years.

"It's after six," Rosie says to Wally. "We should go." They are going out to celebrate their year-and-a-half Anniversary. It will be the first time they've gone out alone since the bigger baby was born.

"Okay?" Rosie says. Wally ignores her and squats beside the tiny, wheezing baby. He jingles the small silver bells tied to each corner of the wash basket. He rearranges the blankets, and strokes the baby's cheek with his heavy hand.

The wheezing tapers away. The baby takes a deep, troubled breath, then sighs.

"Okay," Wally says, straightening.

The baby in Meryl's arms lunges toward the sound of his voice. Meryl catches the baby but drops her cigarette. She snuffs it into the linoleum with her foot, hoping Rosie hasn't noticed.

But Rosie's eyes are on Wally.

"Okay," she repeats, and follows him out the door toward the truck, grabbing their thick coats off the kitchen table as she goes past.

"Bye!" Meryl calls after them, relieved. She bumps the door shut behind them with her hip, holding the bigger baby under the armpits with both hands. The baby kicks and its diaper crackles. *You better not mess,* Meryl thinks. *I'm not changing any diapers.*

She sits the baby next to the other baby in the wash basket and goes from room to room, flipping on lights. She nudges the thermostat from sixty degrees to seventy. Then she calls Jason from the phone in Rosie and Wally's lavender bedroom.

"They gone?" he says.

"Yes."

"I'll be over," he says. His voice is sweet and shy. "Say again where it is?"

She gives him directions, then hangs up and goes back into the kitchen. The bigger baby is lying down next to the littler one. Both of their faces are sprinkled with rash. The bigger baby looks at Meryl dully. The littler baby closes its mouth over its fist.

Rosie told Meryl what sex was like the summer Meryl was twelve and Rosie was sixteen. That summer, Meryl had stayed with Rosie and her mother while her own mother underwent a hysterectomy and her father was in Europe on business. Rosie's mother told Meryl disease of the womb was caused by sin. She thumbed cold holy water crosses on Meryl's forehead, because Meryl had never been baptized. She took Meryl along to Mass each Sunday and let her light a candle for Rosie's father, John, who had died of salmonella. Meryl thought that candle was the most beautiful thing she'd ever seen.

"Sex," Rosie had explained, "is like one of those dreams where you're falling and falling, except in dreams you never hit the ground. With sex, you hit the ground."

Meryl gets her purse and stands in front of the full-length mirror tacked to the back of Rosie and Wally's bedroom door. She combs her hair and puts lime-green make-up over her eyes. She looks at her body from the front, the sides, the back, and draws her belt a notch tighter.

Poor Rosie, Meryl thinks. She and Rosie used to hang around together before Rosie dropped out of high school. Rosie dressed wild then and dyed her hair the color of pumpkin pie. On Saturday nights, she'd grab the mike at Tiny Joe's between sets and holler out stuff at the men.

"Look at this body and weep," she'd say.

Now Rosie is shy. Her hair is short and thin, the color of dry leaves. She gets up early Sunday mornings so she can go to six thirty Mass and be home before Wally and the babies want their breakfast. When she talks her voice rattles, like a hinge on a door that hasn't been used for a long time. *Do you think it's my fault about the baby being retarded?* she asks. *I think it's maybe my fault.*

Meryl goes back into Rosie and Wally's bedroom and lies down on the bed. The smell of the pillows reminds her of stale dough. She grabs a large bottle of sweet perfume off the nightstand and dabs it on her wrists, her shoulders, between her breasts.

Rosie and Wally's bedroom has lavender-colored carpeting and matching lavender curtains. The walls are also lavender, with plum stencils around the ceiling in the shape of little hearts. The bedspread is lavender with great, blue swirls. Blue is Meryl's favorite color, and she traces the swirls with her finger, lying on the bed, smoking Rosie's cigarettes and waiting for Jason.

Blue is the color of the veil on the statue of the Virgin that Meryl has hidden at home in her closet. The closet is the large walk-in kind, and in the crawl space behind her dresses and coats and shoes, Meryl has erected a small shrine. She has, in addition to Mary, a big Jesus, two baby Jesuses, a crucifix, a Joseph, a pious-looking donkey, and a Rosary given to her by Rosie's mother for her sixteenth birthday. Her own mother gave her a box of condoms and pamphlets on sexuality.

How gross! Meryl's friend, Marcy, said when Meryl told her about it at school. Meryl flushed the color of a bruise. They blew the condoms up like balloons and left them in the girls' room drifting lazily over the floor.

Marcy is eighteen and engaged to a fireman named Todd. Todd is twenty-two and *experienced;* Meryl can hardly sit still when Marcy talks about him in her low, delicious whisper. Marcy walks to Confession every Saturday afternoon, and afterward, she comes over to Meryl's house and lies on Meryl's bed and cries. Sometimes, Meryl cries with her. There are things God wants and things people want, and it's hard to know what to do. After Marcy leaves, Meryl sits in her closet, fingering her statues, and tries not to think about anything.

Meryl stole her collection of statues last Christmas, piece by piece, from nativity scenes in grocery stores and malls and doctors' offices. The crucifix she found in an old trunk of her mother's, carefully packed between a prom dress and two orange-and-yellow pom-poms. Before she goes to sleep each night, Meryl crawls into her closet, kisses the crucifix, and prays.

Her mother would die if she knew. Meryl's mother is a Flaming Liberal, a Ball-Busting Feminist, a Bleeding Heart. She tells Meryl that God is something unhappy people create for themselves, that Meryl is free to make her own choices. *My choice is salvation,* Meryl snaps. She wishes her mother would leave her alone.

Meryl cannot forgive her mother for denying her own child the knowledge of God. Rosie's mother says that Meryl shouldn't judge; her mother's soul is in God's hands, and God is merciful and good. But Meryl knows that her mother is wrong, and if you do the wrong thing, you deserve to be punished, unless, of course, you do penance.

Penance, Meryl believes, is important.

Jason's truck squalls up the driveway, tires spinning hard on abrupt patches of ice. Meryl squashes her cigarette and gets up to let him in. He has a twelve-pack tucked beneath his arm and when he kisses her, she smells the cold March air.

"So this is the big night," Jason says. His voice squeaks a little.

"Yes."

"We're really going to do it this time."

"Yes."

"Don't be scared." He looks terrified.

"I'm not," Meryl says, and she gives him a hug. She tugs two beers off the twelve-pack and puts the rest in the refrigerator. Jason peels off his coat and throws it on the kitchen table. He peers into the wash basket.

"Good God," he says.

"What?"

"What's wrong with that one?"

Meryl looks into the wash basket. The bigger baby is asleep, but the littler one is staring at him with its long, wise eyes.

"Mongoloid," says Meryl.

Jason chews the knuckle of his index finger. "That run in your family?"

"Rosie mixed aspirin and beer when she was pregnant. She had a headache and took some aspirin, but then she forgot and drank some beer."

"Wow."

"Rosie's mother thinks that's what did it. It's just a freak thing. It's not in our family genes or anything."

Jason looks at Meryl solemnly. He says, "When *we* get married and have *our* baby, you can't take any aspirin."

Meryl's loves to hear Jason talk about the future. Her heart curls tight with love.

They drink their beers and then drink two more, rapidly, nervously. The bigger baby cries and Meryl gives it a bottle of apple juice. Then Jason opens two more beers and gives them both to Meryl. He slides his hands up under her sweater and Meryl puts her arms around him, still holding the beers, which bump together behind his head.

Beer bubbles down the back of his neck, and he pulls away and gives her a look as though he thinks she might have done it on purpose.

"Sorry," she says.

"It's okay," he says quickly. He takes her hand and leads her into the bedroom. The lavender walls and carpet are a soft, smooth weight bearing Meryl down onto the bed. She kicks off the blue-swirled bedspread because blue is a holy color, the color of Mary, and what Meryl is about to do is sin.

Jason pulls off his shirt. His stomach muscles make little neat rows of boxes, like windows on a tall building.

"Do you have protection?" he says.

"Yes."

"Well," he says. He takes off his jeans. What happens leaves Meryl with a keens sense of shame and an even keener, sharper sense of pride. Afterward, Jason is pale with relief. He presses his face into her breast like a newborn child, and Meryl imagines Rosie's breasts, sticky with milk, and the painful way she carries them.

"Do you know how much I love you?" Jason mumbles.

"Yes."

He is falling asleep. Rosie and Wally won't be back until after midnight, so Meryl doesn't wake him. She is seized by a sudden, wild energy. She struggles out from under him and kisses his soft, open mouth. Then she goes to the bathroom to pee. It hurts, and she shivers; her urine is pale pink.

When Meryl comes out of the bathroom, she hears the thin, shrill wheeze of the littler baby. She feels dizzy from the beer, but she puts on her underwear and Jason's shirt and goes into the kitchen. The radiators hiss and the air is warm, much warmer than in the bedroom. She picks up the littler baby. It swallows and stops wheezing, studies her with its long, wise eyes. She sits in a kitchen chair and rocks it gently with the top half of her body.

Meryl has lied to Jason: she did not have any protection. It is wrong to interfere with God's will, and she will explain that to him, if necessary, if the time ever comes. She thinks about his sperm congealing into a child somewhere deep inside her body, and that imaginary child has Meryl's eyes and mouth and limbs and guts, leaving Meryl with nothing that belongs to her own self at all.

"I'll give up swearing," she begs the walls of the kitchen. "I won't smoke anymore. I'll baby-sit for Rosie for free."

She starts to cry.

The bigger baby awakens and wails, a full-throated bitter cry. Meryl picks it up and balances it with the littler baby in her lap. She and the bigger baby cry and cry in the warm, bright kitchen, but the littler baby is silent. Its eyes are like two planets, glistening and peaceful, somewhere far away and beautiful, the way Meryl imagines Heaven.

He'd seen the woman walking in her yard at twilight, the long neck of a beer trapped carelessly between her fingers and tapping at the faded thigh of her jeans as she picked her way through the overgrown flower beds, the vegetable garden choked with goosefoot and plantain, the old apple trees webbed white with busy tent worms. Once, when she seemed to be looking in his direction, he'd waved to her and his ten-year-old daughter, Julianna, waved too. But the woman dropped her chin and turned her body away as if this were the first time she had realized she might be seen. *Some people are private,* he'd explained to Julianna, placing his broad hand so it spanned her shoulder blades, guiding her toward their own house. After that, he pretended not to see his neighbor on those cool evenings after supper when he and Adelaide drank iced tea on the porch, and Julianna did cartwheels and round-offs and handsprings on the lawn, trilling *Look at me! Look at me!*

He noticed that sometimes she came out of her house with her short hair wet, as if from the shower, and that sometimes her hair was covered by a kerchief which made her head look small, hard, misshapen as the tiny green apples that dropped from her trees and landed on their side of the lot line. He and Adelaide had just bought this house in the spring; they'd spent weeks digging thistles out of the lawn, burning tent worm nests, poisoning the bawdy faces of the dandelions. Adelaide trimmed the shrubs and pulled weeds from beneath them while he and Julianna planted marigolds along the concrete drive, in the flower boxes jutting from the windows like stubborn chins, around the base of the umbrella-shaped maple that opened its deep shade over the house. As the summer passed, and he watched the whimsical drift of dandelion seeds from the woman's yard into their own, he began to feel a clean pinch of irritation that so much hard work could be so easily undone. Her property was an eyesore, the lawn a sunken field of chicory and Queen Anne's lace, strewn with dead branches, broken kitchen chairs, a picnic table turned on its side. Laundry shivered on the line for days, cotton underwear in primary colors, torn T-shirts, pair after pair of limp blue jeans.

One night, as he and Adelaide were settling in between cotton sheets deliciously cool from the air conditioning, she said, "Do you know, I heard the saddest thing about that young woman next door."

It was their habit at night, as they lay drowsing against each other, that she would talk and he would listen until she fell asleep, frequently midsentence, the shape of her last word still faintly on her lips. He trusted her in the way a person without a sense of direction must trust a good map, for he had no understanding of people. But Adelaide knew how to reach beneath the glassy surface of silences and words, select a few careful details and, from these bald scraps, piece out the complex tapestry of a story.

Now she turned to face him, pressed her lips to the edge of his cheek. The woman next door had believed in faith healing and she'd married a man who believed in faith healing, too. They planted their yard in a fiery tangle of tiger lilies, day lilies, dahlias, and zinnias, and evenings after supper they would kneel in the beds, shoulder to shoulder, easing the long roots of weeds from deep between the blossoms. When the man discovered the tumors in his groin and beneath his arms, the driveway filled with cars belonging to members of their church. On weekends they prayed into the night, often not leaving until dawn. Once, the man—in terrible pain—asked to be taken to a hospital, but his young wife talked him out of it, and she cared for him until he died. His relatives, even now, refused to speak to her.

"Can you imagine," Adelaide's breath left a moist coin on his cheek, "how it would be to believe in something that strongly, to be so absolutely sure the way she must have been sure? And every night, after all the visitors had gone, she would have prayed alone, listening for something to tell her she was right, and even though she never heard anything she kept on believing anyway."

When Adelaide didn't say anything more, he realized she was sleeping, her face like a pale smooth stone. He did not like the story she had told him. If the woman next door had truly loved her husband, she would have taken him to a hospital. You did not have to be a psychologist to figure that out. As far as he was concerned, the woman next door was guilty of murder. He got out of bed and walked down the hall to Julianna's room where he found her sleeping on the floor between the bed and the wall. No matter how many times they arranged her properly between the sheets, they found her on the carpeting, frail as a stick, wrapped in her unicorn bedspread. He slipped his hands beneath her and lifted her limp body onto the mattress. Her long legs fell open and one arm was bent awkwardly under her, making the ball of her shoulder stand out like a fist. The half-moons of her fingernails were impossibly white. She sighed, and it seemed that too much time passed before she continued breathing.

She had come home from school one day in spring with a small rectangular picture of Jesus. If you turned the picture in your hand, Jesus spread his arms wide as though he wanted to box your ears, or, perhaps, yell Boo. "I've been saved," she announced, throwing herself backward into a kitchen chair and kicking off the pointy-toed school shoes with the bows she insisted all the girls were wearing. She was starting to worry more about her appearance; Adelaide had found two lipsticks in the backpack she carried to school. "If you don't get saved, you burn in hell." She studied him carefully. He was making meat loaf, shredding stale bread into a pound of ground chuck. They'd just closed on the new house, and half-packed boxes lined the countertops. More boxes, already labeled and sealed, were stacked in front of the cupboards. "Get me an egg," he told Julianna.

She went to the refrigerator and selected one with Adelaide's careful precision, rolling it in her cupped palm as if testing it for ripeness. Then she raised it level with her eyes and stared at it meaningfully. Was she playing a game? He held out his hand impatiently. An egg is an egg, he wanted to say. He wished Adelaide would come home, but it was a Thursday, and she worked late on Thursdays.

"Are you saved?" Julianna asked him.

"Give me the egg," he said, but his daughter swept it behind her back.

"Say, I accept Jesus Christ as my Savior. That's all you have to do, just say it."

This was absolutely ridiculous. She was just a little girl and he was a big man and it would be so easy to spin her around and take the egg away from her—didn't she know that? Or maybe he should just go to the refrigerator and get another egg. But then he'd be letting her have her way. He'd be reinforcing this kind of behavior. He stared into her face, but he could read nothing there except Adelaide's deep-set eyes, his own hard, square chin.

"Give me the egg," he said again.

"Not until you say it."

Adelaide had grown up in a religious home; her parents, devout Catholics, would occasionally slip Julianna a rosary, or a prayer card, or a tiny silver medallion to wear around her neck, and then there would be several days of anxious questions: What is God like? What is sin? Why don't we go to church? Adelaide would take Julianna into her lap and explain that there were many religions and when she grew up she might choose to believe in one of them, or all of them, or none of them, but the choice would be her own.

So he said, "People should be free to choose what they believe in," hoping that would be the end of it. A red flush crept over Julianna's face and she opened her mouth, then closed it with a click. "Just say it," she hissed through her teeth, "you need to say it."

He was tired, over-hungry. "Give me the egg, that's enough, now!" he said, reaching for her arm, but instead of twisting away she dodged toward him and threw the egg at his feet. It shattered, a bright skid of yolk. "Then you'll die," she screamed, "and it will be all your fault!" She dashed out of the kitchen and up the stairs to her room, the slap of the door hollowing his stomach like a punch.

For weeks after that, Julianna belonged to God, but since the move she'd become their daughter again and the small, writhing picture of Jesus had disappeared, he hoped, forever. Now he pulled the sheet up over her and she rolled immediately, as he had known she would, cocooning herself inside it. What children like best, Adelaide said, are safe spaces, firm boundaries, rules that are carefully explained. He kissed his daughter's cheek, tasting salt and a vague bitterness he'd never noticed when she was younger. As he crept back to his bedroom, the floorboards groaned beneath his weight like the sound of someone in pain. Like the sound of someone dying.

Adelaide had unfolded in the center of the bed, a starfish, a cross; she'd forgotten to take off her watch, and its round face beamed on her wrist. He wondered where she'd heard the story she'd told about the woman next door. Perhaps it wasn't true. Perhaps it had been exaggerated. He lifted his bathrobe from the hook behind the door and went downstairs to the kitchen, where he drank apple juice straight from the carton. He realized, for the first time, that he could hear the interstate winding through the valley, over a mile away. *So much for a country setting,* he thought, and suddenly he ached with disappointment. Perhaps they should not have bought this house. Perhaps, if they'd waited just a little longer, something better would have come along.

The moon was full and bright. Through the window, he could see his neighbor's yard, the pale orbs of apples hanging like stars from her trees and glittering on the grass. The picnic table seemed to be reaching like a flat, creased palm from the weeds. He wondered how her husband had felt at the moment he realized his life would not be saved, and then he began to calculate what it would cost to build a privacy fence. Sitting at the kitchen table, he sketched it over and over in his mind until he began to feel better. Until every last detail was right.

Neighbor

G eraldine gets up to let the dog out at five. She steps onto the stoop and stares down at the road, at the swan curve of the street lamp pouring all that light over nothing. It is winter; she wears long johns and gray wool socks that belong to her husband, Lou. Her hair is short and brittle from the perm her sister gave her, thinning a bit on top. When the white tail of the dog disappears into the field, Geraldine goes back inside, crawls deep into the heaviness of Lou's sleep.

At seven, she hears Lou cursing out in the drive. His voice is muffled; at first she thinks it is one of the kids crying, maybe hurt. She gets up and looks between the frost angels on the window.

"Jesus," she says. She raps her knuckles on the glass. Lou has a dead doe by the legs and is dragging her over the ice. She's good sized, still fat with summer, and he rolls her into the culvert. Geraldine grabs her robe, throws it on over her long johns, and runs through the kitchen where the kids are getting breakfast.

"Daddy hit a deer," Timmy says. He's sitting at the picnic table, scooping raspberry filling from the sweet rolls with his finger.

"Jesus," Geraldine says again. She opens the door and steps out onto the stoop.

"Truck okay?" she yells at Lou, clouds of her breath hanging in the air. Her voice is rough with sleep. Lou's already in the cab; he waves, it must be all right. There's blood at the foot of the drive, and the blood looks like a patch of black ice until Lou backs through it and heads off toward his job at Gehl. The wind gusts up a smattering of snow. Geraldine comes back inside and slams the door.

John says, "Dad didn't hit it, somebody else did. It was there when we got up."

97

"He hit it," Timmy says.

Geraldine can tell he wants him to have hit it. "Did he hit it?" she asks Deborah.

Deborah shakes her head no. Deborah is the oldest, a freshman in high school. She is reading a novel over her cereal. The cover of the novel is poppy colored, with a picture of a woman in pioneer clothes clinging to the neck of a cowboy. The title of the novel is *Truest Love*.

"Put that away," Geraldine says.

Deborah's mouth moves, but she keeps reading. The boys have Geraldine's place already set for her: bowl, sweet roll, a glass for Kool-Aid, a spoon. The dog scratches at the door to get in. Geraldine sits down, crosses herself; the boys do, too. The three of them say Grace while Deborah ignores them.

"If you don't take the time for God," Geraldine tells her, "He won't take the time for you when you need Him."

"I am an atheist," Deborah says. "How many times do I have to tell you?"

"There's no such thing as an atheist," Geraldine says. She bites into her sweet roll, then jerks her chin toward the door. "Let the dog in. You, John," she says, and John gets up and does it.

"Yuck!" he says, and Deborah says, "That dog is the *grossest* animal!" The dog's muzzle is smeared with blood; his white bib and paws are flamingo pink.

"Clark's been *eating* it!" Timmy says.

"Shut up," Deborah says. Her voice is knotted, thick, as though she is on the verge of tears. The dog licks its muzzle; the brakes of the school bus creak at the foot of the drive.

"Hurry," Geraldine says, but there is no need to say it. John scoops up both his lunch and Timmy's, they all get their coats and backpacks from the hooks behind the door.

"I'm coming home late with Pete's mom, okay?" John says, and he's out the door quick before Geraldine can say no. Tim and the dog rush after him so there's only Deborah standing in the doorway.

"Ma," she says in her knotted voice, "I can't *live* in a house with a killed deer in the driveway."

Her acne stands out on her forehead. She's a chunky girl, with short bowed legs and hair that won't grow long no matter what she puts on it. Her eyes are glassy and red.

"To get along in this world," Geraldine snaps, "you better stop taking everything so serious."

Deborah whirls, slips, then walks gingerly down the icy drive toward the bus. Geraldine runs her fingers through her brittle hair. It is seven forty-five and already she is tired. She puts on water for instant coffee. She wants to feel sorry for Deborah, but mostly she feels relieved she is gone. Clark scratches at the door; Geraldine doesn't let him in.

The walls of the kitchen are papered with a yellow sunflower pattern. The table is an old picnic table, also papered with sunflowers; above it two windows, bright with ice, overlook the field. The warmest spot in the kitchen is the corner by the radiator where a thin wool blanket lies folded into fours for Clark. Clark is Lou's dog, his baby; at night, he sleeps on Lou's side of the bed.

Geraldine clears away the breakfast dishes and washes them in the double sink. Her socks stick to the linoleum. Clark scratches at the door. Geraldine goes into the bedroom, takes off her robe, and pulls jeans and a sweatshirt over her long johns. The bedroom smells of Clark and Lou; she makes the bed, picks up Lou's clothes, hangs up her robe. With her thumb she wipes dust from the arms of the crucifix hanging above the bed.

Then she goes back into the kitchen and calls her sister, Jill, to see if she wants the deer. Outside, Clark whines and barks.

"It's fresh," Geraldine says. "When I went to let the dog out early I don't remember it there."

"You don't want it?" says Jill.

Geraldine shakes her head into the receiver. "Lou's got the freezer full from his buck. Plus, we got all those ducks down cellar."

99

"Sure," Jill says. "Okay. I'll send Mike over on his lunch break." Mike is Jill's new husband, her fourth; Geraldine is glad their mother didn't live to see it.

"Huh!" Geraldine says. "That Mike won't be able to lift her."

Jill's voice gets stiff. "He'll manage it."

Geraldine hangs up; it's ten o'clock, time for "The Price is Right." Clark scratches at the door, and she tucks the sound far back in her mind. When the phone rings, she has just guessed the price of a whirlpool spa.

"Yes," she says.

"It's Lou."

"I could've won us a spa," she says. "If I was on "The Price is Right" once a year, we'd be millionaires."

"I'm not at work," Lou says. "I just called to tell you."

"You sick? Where are you?"

"Hustesford. I'm at a diner, they let me use the phone. I stopped for coffee."

"Hustesford's an hour away!"

"Fifty-three miles," Lou says. "I thought you should know. I'm not coming back, but it isn't you, or me, or anything personal. I'm just not coming back."

"What?"

"I thought you should know," Lou says, and as he hangs up, Geraldine can *see* him, the way he is bent across the counter, the phone cord stretching between white coffee cups, bread crusts, crumpled napkins, cigarette butts. He is wearing his red-checked hunting jacket, too short at the sleeves. His eyes squint hard against the haze of cigarette smoke, looking, but not at anything in particular, the way he does at night when Geraldine says, *Are you coming to bed?* and he says, *Not yet, Hon. Not just yet.*

100   Geraldine opens the door and Clark shoulders his way inside. His big tail whips her legs. "Go lie down," she says, louder than she means to;

she must think what to do. She sits down on the couch and watches the rest of "The Price is Right" with Clark's heavy head on her foot. The grand prize is a cruise to Alaska. Geraldine can't think of anywhere she'd like to go less; she can see all the snow she wants from her window.

She and Lou had gone for a cruise once, out on Lake Michigan. It had lasted four hours, and there was dinner and a band. Geraldine was pregnant with Deborah, but she didn't know that at the time, and she and Lou got drunk as when they were dating, maybe drunker. The other couples there were no fun at all; they sipped their wine and stared when Geraldine jumped up from the table and started to dance on the empty dance floor. A few of the men kissed their fingers and whistled.

"I got a bug on my ass, or what?" Geraldine yelled. Sweat ran down the sides of her face. "What're *you* looking at?"

"Naw," Lou said, and he got up to join her. "No bugs here. You wanna see? Show 'em, honey," he said, and Geraldine bent low, lifted her skirt, wagged her butt in the air.

The phone rings, and she shoves Clark away. He beats her into the kitchen, and she has to lunge over him to get the phone.

"I hear Clark," Lou says. "Promise you'll let him in at night. I don't want him sleeping outside."

"Lou, where are you going?" Geraldine says. "Where are you going to stay tonight?"

"I'm almost to the Dells. I guess I can sleep in the truck when I get tired, or maybe a motel, I don't know. You know, I haven't really thought about it."

"What'll I do without the truck? What am I going to do, Lou, you tell me that!"

"I'm at one of those Sonny's restaurants. Remember when we used to eat at Sonny's?"

"And tonight when the kids get home I'm going to tell them *what*?"

"They serve breakfast all day," says Lou. "I just want you to know, I left you all the money. I took two hundred dollars and the truck, Gerr, that's it. I want to be fair."

Clark rears up on his hind legs, plants his paws on Geraldine's shoulders, knocks her against the wall.

"Clark, DOWN!" Geraldine yells. Lou has hung up the phone. She swings the receiver by the cord and whacks Clark across the back. He drops down, confused. She whacks him again. She does it hard.

Mike comes by for the doe at noon. He drags her up out of the culvert and stands with his legs spread, resting, hands on his wide hips. Then he turns and comes up the drive, onto the porch, rings the bell. Clark woofs, paws the doorknob. When Geraldine opens the door, he dashes outside.

"Could use a hand getting her up on the truck," Mike says. He is a big man but soft; soft as butter. His eyes are round and too wide.

"All right," says Geraldine, "but it's got to be quick, I'm waiting on a phone call."

"So, Sis, who's supposed to call you?"

Geraldine tugs on her boots, wraps a scarf around her neck. " 'The Price is Right,' " she says. "I may very well be the next contestant."

"Har, har," Mike says. He follows Geraldine outdoors and together they hoist the doe into the back of his truck as Clark dances circles in the snow. The doe's shiny eyes reflect the trees. Its tongue protrudes, a dark red smear.

"I admire a strong woman, Sis," Mike says. "I always did, even before the women's liberation." He follows her back inside the house and Geraldine knows she is stuck with him. She shuts Clark outside, ignoring his wistful stare.

"Don't you have to be at work?"

Mike pulls up his sleeve to check his watch. The hairs on his arm are fine as baby hairs. "Not for another thirty minutes, Sis. Y'know," he says, "I ain't eaten, how about yourself?"

"There's canned soup and peanut butter sandwiches."

"That's grand," Mike says. "And some coffee if you got it."

Geraldine takes off her scarf. She warms the soup and sets the table. Mike gets in her way, standing too close; his breath on her cheek is grim.

"You gonna be on 'The Price is Right'? Well, I've never known a movie star before!"

As she leans over him to pour his soup, he lightly pats her bottom. She takes her own bowl over to the stove and eats there, standing up, as far away from him as she can get. Mike's smile flinches, he wipes his lips.

"Aw, Sis," he says, "I didn't mean nothing by it."

Geraldine vacuums the kids' bedrooms, throwing everything she finds on the floor into a big box in the hall. Then she puts away the vacuum cleaner and takes the box down cellar. She has warned them about leaving their things on the floor; she will tell them she gave it all away to St. Vincent DePaul's. Her face is flushed and angry.

The phone rings just as she comes up from the cellar. Clark moans in his sleep by the radiator; Geraldine hooks the receiver.

"This isn't fair," she says. "You could have warned me. We could have tried to talk about it."

"I'm in Minnesota," Lou says. "Rochester. Is it snowing out by you?"

"A little."

"There's a blizzard here," Lou says. "Real bad. Listen on the radio, see if you hear anything."

"Mike was over to get that doe. He had his hands all over me."

"I think I might try to make it up to Minneapolis. I always wanted to have a look, they say it's clean, not the least bit like Chicago."

"Did you hear me?"

"Honey," Lou says.

"I suppose you got some gal there with you? Is that what this is all about?"

"No," Lou says. He laughs. "But I know Mike's had an eye on you for a while now. I guess you're free to do whatever you want about it."

He hangs up before she can answer.

"Dear God," says Geraldine. There is a horrible, sick feeling inside her and she tries for a moment to pray. Prayer has always helped her think clearly, but now nothing comes to her, not even a loneliness for Lou. She can only imagine how it will be to call Jill and tell her about Lou, and listen to the smugness, thick as soup, in Jill's voice.

Deborah and Timmy get home at three thirty. Clark jumps up at their faces; his testicles bounce, snap back against his belly. Timmy's right eye is swollen and pink. He lets his pack drop to the floor and Deborah grabs it, hangs it on its hook. Geraldine boils macaroni for a casserole.

"He's sick, Ma," Deborah says. She puts her hand on his shoulder, scratches around the blade. She is kind to sick, hurt things.

"Sick how?" Geraldine says.

Timmy raises his head. Deborah takes off her coat and opens the refrigerator. She closes it without taking anything and heads through the living room toward her bedroom.

"That's pink eye," Geraldine says. "There been any other kids sick with it too?"

Timmy shrugs.

"Don't touch your eye," she says. "And don't touch the good one either, or that one will get sick too. Okay?"

Timmy's hand moves up toward his face.

"*Don't* touch it!"

"I'm not touching it, I'm touching my cheek," Timmy says. "It feels funny."

"Go watch TV, get your mind off it. If it isn't better tomorrow, I'll take you in to the clinic."

Timmy goes into the living room and lies down on the couch. Without the truck, Geraldine has no way to the clinic. Or to the store for groceries. Or to St. Michael's for Mass, or to the post office, or over to Jill's or anywhere. She strains the macaroni, throws it into a casserole dish with tuna fish, bread crumbs, milk, and pepper. The TV is shrill in the background. Clark drools, smelling the tuna.

Deborah charges into the kitchen. Her face is pale, her lips bitten white.

"Where's my stuff?" she says. "What did you do with my stuff?"

Geraldine uses her hands to mix the casserole. "What did I tell you about leaving things on the floor?"

"Where's my stuff?" Deborah screams.

Geraldine lets loose with a fistful of tuna casserole. It smacks against Deborah's forehead, slips to the floor; Clark is right there, lapping away. Deborah bursts into tears.

"Whatever is the matter," Geraldine says, the words tight between her teeth, "I wouldn't bother me about it right now."

She goes back to the casserole; Deborah runs to her room.

"Dinner's at five thirty sharp," Geraldine calls after her. "Miss, you better be here."

She rinses her hands in the sink and puts the casserole in the oven. Above the blare of the TV, she can hear Timmy in the boys' room wailing, "Ma, my stuff! What did you do with all of my stuff?" The odd thing is, she doesn't exactly remember.

John gets home at five forty-five, fifteen minutes into dinner. Geraldine and Timmy are picking at small helpings of burned tuna casserole. Deborah is reading another novel; this one is called *Forever*. Clark is under the table, his tail poking up between the chairs like the fin of a shark.

John takes off his coat and washes his hands in the sink. "Sorry I'm late," he says.

Nobody says anything.

"Hey," he says, "What's going on? Where's Dad?"

"He's going to be very late tonight," Timmy finally says. His inflection is Geraldine's.

"What's wrong with your eye?"

"He's sick," Geraldine says. "Pink eye. I don't want none of you touching your eyes, is that understood?"

The phone rings. Deborah rises, but drops back into her seat at Geraldine's look.

"What's wrong with *her*?" John says, stage whisper. Geraldine picks up the phone, turns away from the table.

"I'm almost to Minneapolis," Lou says. "Visibility's real bad. We're going thirty-five on the interstate."

"Timmy's sick," Geraldine says. "Now how I am going to get him to the clinic without the truck?"

She can feel the kids stiffen behind her.

"Call Jill," Lou says. "Jill will take you. What's wrong with Timmy?"

"I can't call Jill. I can't call anybody, Lou, don't you know that? Don't you know what people are going to *say*?"

"Is Timmy really sick?"

"God . . . *Damn* you, Lou," Geraldine says, and hangs up the phone. They all stare at her, even Clark.

"Don't ask me anything," Geraldine says. "Don't."

She picks up the phone and dials Jill. The kids look at their plates. Their faces tell nothing, yellowish from the sunflower reflection of the wallpaper. Timmy's swollen eye weeps and he raises his hand to rub it, checks himself.

"Did you say Grace?" he whispers to John.

John makes the sign of the cross, squinching his eyes tight.

"It won't help you any," Deborah says.

Lessons

t was down by the creek in back of the school where the flowers grew big as cow's eyes, and you maybe picked some of those flowers to smell their green smell, to fill your nose with that smell, while you waited. Horses came there to drink, the old ones left to pasture, and the bones beneath their skin were like lace. There were willow trees and wild strawberries. There were long-legged birds, hopping rock to rock.

I first heard about it when I was in seventh grade. Marsha had gone and so had Karen and Emily and Melissa Ann. You have to protect yourself, now you can get a baby, they said. You don't want to look dumb, fumbling around on dates, cuz if you fumble around they'll know you're cherry and they won't leave you alone till they get it.

It cost five dollars, but I had the money; I had even more money than that from baby-sitting and mowing grass, and I decided to bring it all along with me because I wanted to know everything. I wanted to protect myself. I didn't want to get a baby like Barbie Penco who had to take classes with the grown-ups at night, who walked downtown with her head tucked to her chest and her belly swollen out like a fat old man's.

The lessons were under the bridge, and I went one day late in June. I stood at the top of the embankment and waited while the old horses looked at me with their gummy blue eyes, their flopping lips hanging open. The horses moved toward me, coming over the hill from the barn, coming up from the creek with their stiff legs dark from the water, and they looked at me like they knew everything about me, until I threw a stone to scare them off. The sky was filled with clouds that hung so low they seemed to rest on the backs of the horses as they skittered painfully up the hill and stared at me with their wet lonely eyes.

The boy that came out from under the bridge was a high school boy with a letter jacket. You here for the lessons? he called up to me. I need five dollars up front.

I came down the embankment; it was steeper than I thought, and by the time I got to the bottom I was running to keep my balance.

Relax, okay? the boy said. I gave him the five dollars and he folded it into the pocket of his jeans. Follow me, he said. He had a kind smile.

Under the bridge was another boy, sitting on a stone, and beside him was a girl who was smoking hard on a cigarette. Her hair was crunched into a ponytail that stood up high on her head. She wore earrings in the shape of pumpkins. The boy in the letter jacket pulled down his pants. It looked like lumps.

You ever seen a man's thing before? the girl said. She crushed out her cigarette on the heel of her sandal.

You scared of it? the boy said, and he wriggled it between his fingers. Don't be scared, okay? You learn to do it this way, you'll never get a baby.

The insides of myself became soft and warm and I almost couldn't breathe, but then I could and the softness left and I got mad instead.

I ain't scared of a stupid man's thing, I said, and he burst out laughing and so did the girl and the other boy sitting on the stone. This is what you do, the girl said, and she showed me with her hands. You can't get a baby from doing him like this. Now you try, she said, and I did what she had shown me, swallowing the sick feeling in my throat. Afterward she said, Do you know about protection?

No, I said.

Five more dollars, she said, and I gave her the rest of my money. She showed me a sponge, a condom, foam, and read to me off the packages how to use them. She showed me an empty pill container. You need a prescription for pills, she said, but they work better than anything except what I showed you how to do before. You got any questions? she said, and when I didn't, she said I could go.

You did great, the boy with the letter jacket said. The other boy didn't say anything. I walked back up the embankment picking flowers. I crumbled them in my hands, put their green smell into my mouth. The old horses crowded around me, straining their necks, lifting their swollen feet, nickering, rubbing wet noses on my arms and cheeks, yearning for human touch.

Spot Weaknesses

would like to know what you are thinking. You stand in front of me, arms akimbo, and the sharp, blue points of your elbows make me want to weep. Your body is a series of impossible angles, terrible demands, and beside you I feel swollen and slow, conscious of my breasts and belly and hips, a distortion of your sapling strength, your arch-backed wonder, your high child's stomach. At nine, you already hate that stomach and after school, with your lip-glossed, child-stomached friends, you read magazines I would forbid you to read if I were not still drawn to them myself. On airplanes, in waiting rooms, standing in the grocery store check-out line, I learn how to trim fat from my waist, to accentuate my eyes, to dress in a way that hides what a well-known designer calls *spot weaknesses*. By the time I was nine I kept my feet crossed to conceal my chunky ankles, a suggestion I'd read in what, back then, girls called a *beauty magazine.* I wore the same sweet perfume smuggled to school in my new stiff purse that you are wearing now, though if I confront you, you'll deny that you've ever heard of such a thing—*perfume?*—your arms tightening around the cage of your ribs as if to protect your very heart.

I have said you can ask your two best friends, Rachel and Kendra, for a sleep-over tonight, and the topic of our conversation is pizza. I want to doctor up a store-bought; you want me to order from a pizza parlor that delivers, and not just any pizza parlor but the one in the mall at Murphy's Point where the delivery people wear pizza-shaped hats, the place that charges an additional five dollar fee to come this far into the country. I say that our topic is pizza, but if this were the only thing we are talking about then you wouldn't be looking at me this way. Holding yourself in the vise of your arms. Preventing yourself from falling on the floor and kicking your feet in their grown-up style shoes and curling your pink-chipped fingernails into your palms. Rachel and Kendra are your best friends today, but two weeks ago they decided to hate you. They showed up at our house like deputies with a warrant, unsmiling and businesslike, holding a cardboard box to collect every gift they'd given you since the first day you led them into our home, haughty and beaming and proud. Even now, that box has not been returned. Or perhaps it has, and this is just one more thing I don't know about you and your new private life, which I'm trying so hard to respect because I remember feeling, at nine, that no one respected mine. I know how ashamed you were as you cried and cried yourself nauseous after the girls left. I sat by the toilet, stroking your hair as you choked and gagged, *I don't understand, I didn't do anything. Why are they so mean?*

I remember my own childhood friends, Joy Middleton and Elizabeth Sears, and the first day of fifth grade when I ran to them, eager after a long summer on my own, and they told me they could not speak to me unless I became a member of their club, a club which had only one requirement: members had to have a brother or sister. I was an only child. The girls walked away from me, skirts switching their calves, and I went home and begged my mother for a baby. I told her having just one child was selfish, something I'd overheard a friend's mother say. I told her I hated the way she smelled when she came home from her job plucking hens at the cannery, even though all she ever smelled of was hand lotion, hairspray. I told her our apartment was ugly, our lives were awful, nothing she did ever worked out right.

You explain that the pizza you want me to order is the kind all the cool kids' parents order, parents like Kendra's who allow her and Rachel to spend Saturday afternoons shopping alone in the mall at Murphy's Point. You point out that when I have a *man* over for dinner, I cook things that are special, and now you are only asking for things to be special for your friends, too. I point out that the last *man* I invited for dinner ate store-bought pizza and liked it, but I will excuse you for forgetting because that was over two months ago. And then, because I am tired from work, because I have agreed to an invitation I did not, do not, want to make, I point out that I wouldn't invite a *man* to dinner who was so shallow he decided he liked me or didn't like me based on what we ate.

I watch your face, so full of anger and the power of that anger, and I wonder why you are unable to turn this face on anyone but me. Were you to look at Kendra or Rachel this way, they would melt away like perfect wax dolls, Kendra's smooth cheeks, Rachel's shining hair, until all that was left would be two soft wax stools that could easily be remolded into something else. You would frighten the boys who harass you in the hallways at school and whistle when I arrive—an embarrassment—to pick you up at four thirty. You would have frightened the man who began to accompany you when you were still walking the six blocks home alone. I would have picked you up all along, I told you then, if only you'd said something, honey, I could have done something to stop it.

He was a white male in his late twenties, and the first time you saw him he was sitting on the swings, waiting, he said, for his own little girl who was only in kindergarten. *Not a big girl like you,* he said, *almost grown up already,* and I can imagine how you smiled in your smuggled-in lipstick, your new purse slapping your hip as you walked away. Smaller than the other girls your age, always mistaken for somebody younger. But now this kind man, this father (whatever that means—your own left before you could remember him) knew a good thing when he saw it. A big girl, almost grown up already. After that, you often saw him after school, chatting with the other parents, waiting for his little girl, the one in kindergarten. *But she isn't as pretty as you,* he said. *She doesn't have such pretty hair like yours.*

Did he touch you? was the first thing I asked, and I died, I *lost my life* right there, sitting in the kitchen on the same chairs that had been in my mother's kitchen, when you nodded.

Show me. Show me where. Point with your finger if you can't say.

You raised both your hands—up, up to touch the top of your head, stroking the smooth surface of your hair, and I inhaled, feeling my life snap back into my chest. It was two months ago that I called the police to report that a white male in his late twenties had stalked my nine-year-old daughter for weeks, and I hadn't known—I use to read about things like this and ask myself, Where were the parents?—about it until just now, when she told me he had tried to lure her into his car. A policewoman came and you bravely told her everything you'd told me; how every day he'd walk beside you a little farther, asking about your school work, your hobbies, and were there any boys you particularly liked? He always had to turn back because his daughter, just a kindergartner, would be looking for him, but then, one day she had to stay home with the flu. *Would you like to come visit her?* he asked. *We could stop and get ice cream to cheer her up.* His car was right there, and he opened the door for you, smiling, a gentleman right out of a magazine.

I want to believe you ran because you remembered all my warnings. *Don't talk to strangers. Never accept a ride from someone you don't know.* When you could barely talk, I helped you memorize your name, address, and phone, so that in case you got lost I would be able to find you back. I showed you how to cross the street: *Look left, right, left again.* I gave you a chewable vitamin every morning when the doctor recommended them; I switched to a vitamin tablet when the doctor said all the sugar in the chewables was harmful; I stopped altogether when that same doctor said that vitamins were unnecessary. But you were not thinking about anything I'd ever done or said the afternoon that man held the door open to you. You recognized something in that smile, something far older than you or me, something that whispered beyond your ears and into your blood. You ran all the way home and pounded the door so forcefully that, at first, I was afraid to open it, not imagining it might be you. But it was, your cheeks ribboned with tears, your ears bright with the cold March wind. You shook against my stomach, bending low to put your head where you always tucked it when you were younger, after a fall, a frustration, a scare.

Now you are in your bedroom, face down on your bed, as if you used up every last ounce of your energy giving me that one, long furious look. I touch your back, and your shoulder blades stiffen, poking up like tiny birds' wings. You tell me to go away. You tell me I just don't understand. But I do understand the importance of appearances: the right dress, the right smile, the right kind of parlor pizza. The way we delude ourselves with small details that give an illusion of control. If the pizza is right, the girls will like us. If our stomachs are flat. If our ankles are thin. If I feed you vitamins, instructions, magical phrases like *Don't talk to strangers.*

We compromise on a delivered pizza from a nearby pizza parlor. You'll keep Rachel and Kendra entertained in the living room while I answer the door, slip the pizza onto a platter, discard the cardboard box that betrays its unacceptable origins. You get up and together we clean the house, you washing the dishes with so much detergent it will leave a vague metallic taste behind, me raking the vacuum cleaner over the rug, reminding myself again that I need to rent a good carpet cleaner.

And then the girls arrive, dropped off together by somebody's mother, not a good sign because that means they've had time alone together to plot, to rehearse. But tonight they are cordial, kissing the air behind your ears, something they've copied and you copy back quick, making your own smacking sounds. Nobody moves to kiss me, the Mother, graceless and old and boring with bills and grocery shopping, work and late-night TV. Hello, Mrs. Wells, they say and your eyes are pleading, *Be nice, pretend they weren't mad, pretend that nothing ever happened.* So I smile a crisp hello and suggest they play in the living room—their eyes roll at the word *play*—while I call for pizza.

I watch them from the doorway as they settle on the floor, shoulders touching, long legs folded neatly beneath their thighs. Rachel takes a wad of paper from her pocket, smoothes it open on the floor.

Who's it from? you ask, and when Kendra whispers a name you say, No *way!* I step back into the kitchen so that if you look up, I will not appear to be watching. But the eagerness in your voice hurts me. You are trying so hard, so terribly hard, and there's nothing I can do for you now but step back and hope that the past few months will some-day fall into perspective so that this night, these girls, the false kind-ness of a stranger will drop away, not forgotten but unnecessary. Looking at you, I do not understand why you are the follower, they are the leaders; why they are the ones you will look to for your immediate direction and hope. Already, your head is bending toward them as if you are hoping to learn something vital. As if you are listening for a clue.

Sybil

The twins pat mousse into Sybil's hair, working the tight, carefully blued curls into stiff barbed wires the color of salmon. She cannot escape without her walker, and they have taken her walker down the front steps and across the front lawn to the hickory tree. The mousse stings her scalp. It's strawberry scented, and a myriad of tiny flies circle blindly overhead, lured into the kitchen through the screen door which is propped open by a brick.

"She's crying," says the first twin.

The second twin peers into Sybil's face, small pink mouth agape. Sybil can see a sliver of white in the child's gum where a new tooth is coming in. The twins have lost their top front teeth this summer. *Angel teeth,* their mother calls them.

"No she's not," says the second twin. "She's just thinking, that's all."

"Maybe she's thirsty."

The second twin considers this and goes over to the refrigerator. She takes out a pitcher and pours Kool-Aid into a glass she finds on the counter. She carefully brushes an ant from the rim of the glass. A smoke-gray cat, panting with heat, is coiled between the dishes in the sink. The twin scratches its head. Everything she touches gets kissed with a faint, pink smear of mousse. She holds the Kool-Aid to Sybil's lips, but Sybil turns her face away.

"See?" says the twin. "She don't want anything."

Her sister kisses Sybil's neck. Both twins are solemn little girls with pale yellow cheeks and yellow pony tails and their voices are pinched and whispery. They make more barbed wires with the mousse. They work until every inch of Sybil's head is spiked and rosy.

"She looks bea-u-tee-ful," says the first twin serenely.

"I don't think she likes it."

"She looks just like a movie star."

The second twin drinks the Kool-Aid. They look at their grand-mother with wispy blue eyes, their bright gazes crossing and recross-ing her face the way spotlights search a dark sky.

Margie gets home from work at five, and the first thing she sees is Sybil at the table with spiked, rosy hair. The twins are nowhere in sight. Ants cluster on the table where drops of mousse have fallen.

"Oh, God," says Margie. "Where are they? Where'd they go? Oh, Sybil, I'm so sorry! It washes out, though, I've used it on my bangs. It'll rinse away in a jiffy, I swear."

Sybil tries to form words and strange sounds come from her mouth. The stroke has garbled her speech. When she's calm, she can write the words, gripping a pen with her fist. But Sybil is not calm.

"I've got a *date!* Can you believe it?" Margie says, brushing past Sybil and twisting on the cold water faucet in the sink. The smoke-gray cat hops out onto the countertop. It flicks its paws, one at a time. Margie splashes water on her face. She hasn't had many dates since Victor left four years ago, but she makes the most of what she gets.

"God, this heat, can you believe it? Ninety-five downtown, hotter tomorrow I bet. Johnny Hecht asked me to dinner at The Gander. They got air conditioning and big-screen TV."

Sybil says, "H-H-Hair!"

"Johnny, he don't mind kids, he got his own two anyway. We got talking on lunch today, and he said, 'C'mon, let's get outta here,' so we went mini-golfing at The Palace. You know, that place off I-94? With the big dinosaurs?"

Margie wipes her face and twists a pen into Sybil's hand.

"Write down where they went to," she says. "I gotta get dressed. And don't worry, I promise that'll wash right out."

She trots down the hall toward her bedroom, unbuttoning her uniform as she goes. Margie is a receptionist at The Lakeside Hotel. Sybil's son, Victor, had been the one to hire her. Sybil scrawls HAIR on the formica table top. Fingers of mousse seep down her neck.

Victor disappeared when the twins were three years old, and Sybil knew he'd done the smart thing. By that time, they all were living with her. Sybil thinks they brought on her stroke, but Margie says that's ridiculous.

"You're just lucky we're here," she chirps. "If we weren't, you'd be stuck in a home somewheres."

Margie loves Sybil very much. She tells Sybil, *I love you like my own ma!* and she whispers Sybil things she could never say to anyone. She reminds Sybil of Sybil's own mother, Georgia, who died eleven years ago. Georgia was disorganized. Georgia said she loved people all the time, but it never amounted to anything.

Hair, Sybil writes on the formica. Hair. Hair. Hair.

Margie comes back into the kitchen wearing a red strapless sundress that rides up when she walks. Her body bounces but her hair, stiff with spray, is like a helmet. She yanks down the sundress and leans over to read the formica.

"I know, your hair, but I gotta get your dinner first. Where'd the twins go?"

Sybil draws a question mark.

Margie sighs. She takes a carton of cottage cheese out of the refrigerator, sniffs it, and brings it over to Sybil.

"It's too hot for anything cooked," she says, "and Johnny'll be here any minute."

She sweeps ants off the table with the flat of her hand and spoons cottage cheese into Sybil's mouth. "Johnny knew Victor and he says

Victor was never real responsible. *Johnny's* responsible. He's got two kids of his own, boys, the oldest's just seven. I mean, not to count my chickens, but they'd be good for Trish and Tina, don't you think?"

The smoke-gray cat glides up onto the table and Margie says, "Sybil! Where's your walker?"

Sybil looks out the window.

"Huh? Oh, God, Sybil, I'm sorry. They musta been trying to climb that tree. Here, I'll go get it for you."

She pushes back her chair and trips out the door and down the porch steps. Through the window, Sybil watches her float across the lawn like a large red sun. The smoke-gray cat noses forward. Sybil lifts her arm to wave it away, then lets it drop. The cat's tufted chin sinks into the cottage cheese.

Margie comes in with the walker as a truck pulls into the drive. She squeals, "It's Johnny!" and yanks at her sundress. A heavy-set man with very red skin and white-yellow hair steps out of the truck. Sybil feeds the barbed wire points on her scalp as if they are electrified.

"HAIR!" she chokes.

Margie looks at her, does a double-take.

"Christ, I forgot!"

It's too late: Johnny thumps up the porch steps and swings his head through the doorway.

"Hey," he says to Margie. Then he sees Sybil. His gaze sticks to her, caught in a rosy web of mousse.

"Johnny," says Margie in a grand way. "This is my mother-in-law, Mrs. Kelly."

Margie takes Johnny's arm and her face opens up to him like a flower. Sybil has forgotten how Margie acts when she desperately wants to be pretty. Sybil herself never needed to act: at Margie's age, she'd been something to look at. Still, Johnny's eyes slide from Sybil to rest on Margie's thick waist and calves.

"Mama, you are somethin'," he says.

Margie turns to Sybil, winks, and murmurs, "Get the twins to bed at nine." She and Johnny glide down the porch steps, Johnny's hand on her hip, her hip thrust into his hand.

Sybil's throat feels dry and strange. She pulls herself up on her walker and moves out onto the porch to watch the truck bounce down the drive. The floor of the porch boils with ants. The smoke-gray cat twirls around Sybil's ankles, its tail bolt upright like an exclamation.

Sybil is sixty-eight. When she was forty-one and red-headed and trim, she rode through town shirtless on the back of a Chevy pick-up, eyes tearing, nipples hard as pits. It was dark, but someone must have recognized her because she got arrested outside of Tiny Joe's.

"Mama, you are somethin'," the officer had said, and, drunk as she was then, Sybil still remembers it. Lying in bed, sticky with mousse, she thinks about the coolness of the jail that night where, laughing herself to sleep, she'd had the power to live forever. *Mama, you are somethin'.* It's twelve fifteen and too hot to sleep. Margie has not come home.

Sybil wears the same housecoat she's worn all day. It smells like onions, sour and hot. Its pattern of pink roses is faded almost white, making the length of her body glow eerily in the darkness. The twins are sleeping on the couch in the living room, nestled together like spoons. They told Sybil it's cooler there than in their bedroom, but Sybil knows they just want to watch adult TV and practice kissing on their hands.

A ragged motor works its way up the drive, idles, coughs, and quits. Margie's giggle floats high in the air; two doors slam, and Sybil hears Johnny say, "*Shhh!*" extra-quiet, extra-careful, and she realizes they are drunk and that they mean to come inside. They tumble up the porch steps and into the kitchen. Something falls, shatters.

"Shit," Johnny hisses.

"Don' wake th' babies."

Sybil hopes that Margie will come in to check on her so she can get out of her housecoat and sleep in her panties and bra. But Margie moves past Sybil's room toward her own, Johnny plodding behind her. He stops off at the bathroom and releases a stream that makes Sybil think of horses. Then he goes into Margie's bedroom and shuts the door. The smoke-gray cat appears in Sybil's doorway. It pauses, springs like a shadow onto her bed. When the noises start, it stiffens, sniffing the air in the direction of Margie's bedroom wall. Then it curls up against Sybil's leg, its wide eyes green and knowing.

The twins are up; Sybil can hear them. The hall light clicks on and it's not long before they, too, are in Sybil's room.

"She's awake," the first twin says. "Look, her eyes are open."

"She can't sleep cuz of *them*," says the second twin. She picks up the cat, kisses it, and settles into its place with it tucked into her lap. Sybil can feel the heat coming off of the child's body. The noises in the next room grow louder, and Sybil wishes the child would move away.

"Aawh," she breathes.

The first twin crawls over her chest and sits cross-legged on her pillow. She looks tenderly into Sybil's face.

"What do you want?" she whispers.

Sybil doesn't know. Johnny's husky cries bead sweat like ice across her forehead.

"She wants them to shut up," says the second twin. The cat's ears rotate, radar style. A breeze lifts the curtains, and Sybil feels her whole body breathe that gasp of air.

The noises stop. The twins settle down next to Sybil, one on either side, their legs draped over her legs. A spiked lock of hair dangles across her eyes, and one of the twins, noticing this, sleepily brushes it back. The cat sleeps at their feet, twitchy with dreams.

In the morning, the twins grab Sybil's arms, pulling her upright. She's still asleep, so they help her swing her feet over the side of the bed. They button up her housecoat, rubbing their faces into her arms, patting her hands.

"You kin use the bathroom now," one of them says. "It's empty."

Sybil gropes for her walker and moves painfully down the hall, stiff with morning. She uses the toilet and tries to wipe some of the mousse off her face with a wet washcloth she finds squashed in the sink. When she comes out of the bathroom, the twins are waiting for her. They're uncertain. They slouch against the walls.

"They're in the kitchen," the first twin says. "They're eating breakfast."

"The *man* is here," says the second twin.

Both girls look to Sybil to see what *she's* going to do. Sybil straightens her shoulders and grips her walker. The twins follow behind her, clutching her housecoat, and the three of them move down the hall and into the kitchen. Johnny's at the table with Margie hanging over his shoulder. Margie's got on a T-shirt that's just long enough. From the table up, Johnny looks naked, but Sybil realizes he has jockeys on, lavender jockeys with a paisley print.

Johnny and Margie see Sybil at the same time. The barbed wires on her head have been flattened by sleep, but the color is still true and has spread to her cheeks and neck. Each of the twins has a rosy patina on the side of her head that slept next to Sybil.

"Morning," says Margie, and she and Johnny burst out laughing. They're eating cereal mixed with beer and drinking from a long dark bottle in the center of the table. They go on laughing for a long time. Sybil cannot keep her eyes from the white-yellow hair on Johnny's chest, the hard, rounded mound of his belly. She wants to press her face into his skin.

"Come get your breakfast," Margie says, "and say hello to Johnny. Johnny this is Trish and Tina. And you already met Mrs. Kelly."

Sybil stares at Johnny. Margie tugs her into a chair and fills her mouth with cereal, giving her fresh spoonfuls before she has time to swallow. The twins pick at their Frosty-Pops. Johnny's hands work their way under Margie's shirt; Margie tilts her head back so he can kiss her full on the mouth. Sybil's eyes fix on that kiss. The inside of her mouth fills with water. She wants that kiss to last forever.

"Kiddos, help Gram with her breakfast, okay?"

Margie slides from her chair, and Johnny rises to follow her out of the kitchen. The seat of his jockeys has been worn sheer; Sybil traces the dark flesh-crack with her eyes. She tries to picture the men she has known, but they all disappear into their own laughing mouths and hungry eyes, and she suddenly can't remember if she's ever had a lover at all. The smoke-gray cat skulks into the kitchen, jumps onto the table. It sniffs at a bowl of cereal and beer. When the noises start, its ears fold back like wings.

The twins roll their eyes at each other. They turn to Sybil, but she's reaching for her walker; Sybil can't bear those noises any longer.

"What do you want?" the first twin asks her.

"It's chow time!" says the second twin, and she climbs up onto the counter and reaches into the top cupboard. She pulls down a bag of cookies.

Sybil moves out onto the porch; she can tell by the smell of the air it will be another hot day, with more to come. A twin comes out and nudges a cookie into her hand. As Sybil brings it to her lips, it slips, breaking against the wooden floor of the porch.

"Look what you did," the child says, and her voice and inflection are her mother's. She and Sybil stare at the ribbon of ants that already has formed to carry the pieces away.

The Trial

She was twelve and the man was forty-two. This man was a lawyer with a wife and six children; I knew three of his sons. One of them still lives here in Holly's Field, and he's got two kids of his own. But the girl, that twelve-year-old, she sat in the courtroom and cried. They were arguing whether a twelve-year-old could love anybody. The lawyer did not cry or anything, he just waited. That is what people said about it.

Because the trial was an open trial and everybody knew. The women stayed away, but the men of Holly's Field, including my father, went to the courthouse on their lunch hours and sneaked quick trips in the afternoons. I was one year older than that girl, and the trial went on for a week. The boys talked about it at school, and their foreheads and cheeks turned red if we looked over at them, but it did not stop their talk.

How embarrassed we were to have them talk that way!

At night my father kept a strange, hard light in his eyes. He paced the floor, drank too much beer. His hands moved by themselves in the air.

"It's a sickness," my mother said. She was a beautiful woman with feet the size of a child's. "It's a disease, all of you in that courtroom with your tongues hanging out like dogs."

And—"That poor girl," she said a lot.

"It's all them vitamins nowadays," my father said. "These girls, they grow up early, then they don't know what they want."

I wanted my father to love me. I always took his side. On the third day of the trial, the girl began to wave her arms and scream, *You leave him alone, You leave him alone.* They had two social workers, two ladies in dark suits, who spoke the word *rape* without lowering their heads, and by afternoon that word crept through the halls at school like smoke. Holly's Field is six thousand people and everybody knows everybody, but the boys began to look at us as though we were someone strange, and after school they chased us and called us names that caught hard in our stomachs.

When my father came home for supper that night, the light in his eyes burned brighter. "They say it was rape," he said, "but that girl says it was love."

"That girl is just a baby," my mother said. "You and those men with your tongues hanging out like dogs."

"This is America," my father said. "Marie, this is an open trial and I'll go if I goddamn please."

I was one year older than that girl. My father was forty-eight, and his gaze cut my body into ragged parts and all of those parts were wrong. He wanted so much for me to be beautiful, but I was bow-legged, flat chested, ashamed. That girl was a round, pert little thing, with a squashed pig nose and freckled arms. She carried her books pressed to her chest when she walked through the halls, but her breasts still jiggled beneath them.

Her breasts are what I remember most, as if they caused the whole thing, which some people claim they did. I'm married now to a man who grew up two towns over from Holly's Field. He's a quality inspector at the preserving company, and I am lucky to have this man, a quality inspector, who earns good money and treats me well. With my looks, there were never any lawyers snooping around for me. My father reminds me about that still. He tries to see my mother in me, but the best he can see is himself.

My mother was a beautiful woman with feet the size of a child's. When he married her he could circle her waist with his fingers. Each night before bed he combed out her hair, shining down the length of her back, with a brush made of ivory and carved with her name, *Marie*. My father named me Marie, for my mother. He wanted so much for me to be beautiful.

My mother did not want anything that I could easily see. She lost her hair to cancer and when she died there was not much left to say. My father won't call me Marie anymore; he calls me May or nothing at all. My husband calls me Marie. It is the most beautiful name I know.

That girl, the girl who sat in the courthouse and cried, she doesn't live in Holly's Field anymore. Her family moved to Milwaukee, where her troubles could get swallowed up by other people's troubles. But trouble doesn't quit a person just like that, and it did not quit that girl. She came down with a sex disease, something you don't get rid of, it sticks with you through your life like a fingerprint. His people, the lawyer's, tried to make out that she'd had it to begin with. And many like my father believed it was so. But her people proved the lawyer had had it all along, so the court fined him one thousand dollars and gave him five years probation. His sons still came every day to school; big boys, good with their fists. They called us names that stuck hard in our stomachs and made us squirm with shame.

"Those girls," my father said. His gaze moved over my ragged parts. "They are at that age where they don't know what they want."

"Like dogs," my mother said, "with your tongues hanging out full of drool," and my father almost hit her, but my father never hit a woman in his life, and he did not hit her then. She stayed on with him until she died, and when she died he wept for days. My mother did not want anything I could easily see.

My little girl, she has my looks, so no lawyers will be coming for her either. She is six and my little rainbow. My sunshine, my sweet girl. She climbs all over my father and rubs her sticky fingers in his beard. The court ruled that a twelve-year-old isn't capable of love, but the hard part about that is how much they were wrong. Because love doesn't come according to an age and that is the saddest thing I can think of. And when I look at my daughter and her hands already in my father's beard, I know that to live in this world, I must be reconciled to that.

I remember the year it was rain that we prayed for, the death rattle of the crops our evening lullaby. Mornings, I rose to the dry catch of dust in my throat as the boys coughed themselves awake, rattling the bars of the divider that kept them from wandering out of their room and tumbling down the stairs into Alma's part of the house. I tasted the drifting fields in the damp folds of their necks, in Foster's sour kiss, in the second cup of coffee I drank after he'd left for work, a fawn-colored cloud of dust funneling behind his truck. At noon, we ate lunch with Alma in the coolness of the root cellar, gulping can after can of grape pop and pressing our toes into the damp dirt floor. Alma owned the house outright as well as the sixty acres of land she leased to the canning company. "This heat don't bother me," she said. "I get paid whether they take the crop or no."

"I don't mind it either," I said. "It's like being on vacation in Florida or somewhere."

But each of us knew that the other had lied. There was shame in the terrible thirst of the corn, in the yellowing leaves and withering stems, the waste of it all, the wretched waste, and when the boys ran through the brittle rows at twilight, I shook with the sound of breaking bones.

"Come on out of there! You, Howard! Jamie!" They obeyed, my four-year-old tow-headed boys, born just ten months apart. *Still babies,* Foster liked to say, *too young for anything but belly-aching.*

"Aw, they ain't hurting anything," he said. The dust in the air had kissed the sweat around his mouth; his lips looked made-up, like a woman's. "Crop's gone to shit, the world knows it."

"Don't say that word in front of them," I said.

127

"And which word might that be?" Foster said, his eyes shining innocent gold. The boys laughed because he was laughing. And maybe it was then that it all started, in the dusky heat, with the last faint bloom of summer curling up all around us. Now Howard's thirteen, sprouting hair along his jawbone. Jamie already wears a size twelve shoe. *Foster's boys,* people call them, and it's true—they won't listen to a thing I have to say anymore. They nod, their flat stares scorching my face, but they know the right look from Foster will knock my words from the air like a flock of clay doves. "You leave them boys to me," he says, each word the firing of a gun. And Howard and Jamie aren't about to wait around for me to pick up the pieces.

Today, they are both in a bad morning mood. Neither of them got his homework done, I can see it in their faces, though they both tell me different when I ask. They have to go to make-up class all summer long because they failed their regular school year. "Hustle up," Foster says to them. "I'm leaving at six thirty whether you two are ready or no." They eat and they eat: toast and peanut butter, toast and jelly, sugar doughnuts, cereal with milk, cereal poured dry from the box into their hands. "Manners," I say, but I'm no more than a mosquito's whine in their ear.

"*Man*-ners," Howard hisses to his brother.

"Lick me," Jamie says.

Foster says, "You two better hustle up."

I clear away their dishes, take the last of my coffee to the window where I watch the new sun bloom beyond the fields. It's the first clear morning we've had this month, and the flood waters shine like sheets of ice. I've always been afraid of water. As children, my sister and I took swimming lessons at the lake-front park, but I never got in past my knees. I hated the idea of my foot coming down and not knowing what might be under it. I hated the feeling that something could reach up and grab me that I couldn't see. Now there is water everywhere I look, reflected sky and cotton clouds spread over the ground. On Sundays after the homily, when we kneel down to pray for good dry weather, you can feel how much everyone wants the same thing, and how little we expect to get it.

"Let's go, let's go!" Foster says, clapping his hands, and the boys rocket down the stairs and into the front yard, jumping puddles and scattering the irritable flock of geese, another abandoned 4-H project. The truck is parked in two inches of water; Howard splashes Jamie, Jamie punches Howard. Foster comes up behind me, kisses me hard on the neck. He says, "Get some sleep, Marilee." There are those who envy me, married fourteen years to a man who never forgets to kiss goodbye.

But things have been bad between all of us ever since I started working full time, five nights a week from eight till four thirty, so Foster can go to school. I remember how I used to step into the day like an old familiar dress, and maybe it wasn't beautiful, maybe it wasn't the best I could own, but at least it was mine and I wore it well and I knew how to mend where it tore. By noontime, I'd have the house put right, and I'd go downstairs to Alma. "How're them weeds of yours?" she'd ask, proud of the boys as I was. They'd grown up in her kitchen as much as mine. Summers, they followed us around the vast garden we kept together, picking raspberries and gooseberries and strawberries for canning, running to the shed for a forgotten tool, climbing high into the apple trees to hang the pie tins that scared off birds.

Now I lose each day to a restless, dreamy sleep, and when I get up late in the afternoon, I'm cotton-headed from the drumming of the rain, disoriented, not quite real. It's as if I'm watching someone else fix supper for Foster and the boys, and carry a plate downstairs to Alma, and do up the dishes, and put them away—though of course it's me, who else could it be? Then I drive fifteen miles of washed-out roads to the department store in Cedarton, where I stare at the flickering security screen and try not to think about being alone in the hollowed-out belly of the building. I read magazines or write letters to my sister in Denver; when it gets really bad, I say the Rosary. But all night long I hear noises—the muffled grunt of a window giving way, the thud of a man's heavy boot, the rain on the taut tin rooftop wild as the beating of my heart.

Alma knows just how bad it is, but Foster tells me there's nothing to be afraid of. "Nobody's going to break in," he says. "You're there to keep their property insurance down, that's all." Insurance, profit, risk—these are the things he studies at school, but school can't help him understand this has nothing to do with being afraid and everything to do with fear. And when fear swallows your voice and drinks up your spit and hurts you deep in your privates, you let it have its way. It's what you feel during childhood nightmares, when outrageous things seem like honest possibilities: the two-headed monster, the six-foot-tall lion, they do exist, yes they do, wait here with me and you'll see. Howard and Jamie used to dream the same dreams, just like you hear about with twins. I'd go to their room, flipping on lights, tasting their screams in my own throat. When they buried their faces against me, I remembered the hot wet force of their births, how their crying mouths opened for my breast already knowing and it seemed to me then there was nothing I could teach them.

You'll ruin them boys with that babying, Foster warned me. Some nights, when they cried out for me, he held me down, playfully, not playfully, his tongue stuffing my mouth like a rag, his body inside my body. *Ma!* the boys screamed, I can still hear them. *Oh, Ma!* Now, whenever I come into their room, they stop whatever they've been doing. Their faces are as smooth as the faces of the mannequins I pass on my rounds every night, ruddy complexions hushed by the artificial twilight, not quite real, yet close enough to be believed. Frozen mouths. Staring eyes. They don't even bother to ask, *What do you want?* They are endlessly patient, these mannequin boys with Foster's face and my own cold limbs.

At work, I know all the mannequins by heart—the children holding hands in their back-to-school clothes; the twin hunters dressed in khaki with black grease paint under their eyes; the shapely young mother in Home Appliances; the teenage girl modeling swimwear on a sandy platform in Sports and Recreation. My favorite is the bride in the Young Miss department, unbearably fragile in her white white gown with the sweetheart neckline, the pearly buttons, the lacy train coiled around her feet. I visit all of them, nights, on my rounds, touching their clothing, their hair, their long, smooth jointed fingers, adjusting the little girl's knee-socks, smoothing the teenager's stiff blonde hair. Their mouths are half open, puckered with worry, as if they want to warn me about something only they can see. Their eyes are fixed on it. They cannot look away; they are frozen with a fear I recognize. And then it's like the game I played as a child, imagining someone just behind me, and as long as I don't look I'll be okay. I force myself to finish my rounds before returning to the windowless office at the back, walking as slowly, as deliberately, as I can. The security screen never shows more than the quiet rows of merchandise, the mannequins holding their awkward poses, the vague outline of my face reflected back.

I've called in three false alarms since spring. Max Bolton, the day guard, makes fun of me for it. He phones me on the security channel, breathes heavily in my ear. Sometimes he talks about filthy things. Sometimes he doesn't say anything at all. *Just making sure the bad guys ain't gotcha,* he says when I tell him to knock it off. The tone of his voice lets me know he is smiling in a way that shows all of his sharp, yellow teeth.

When my sister got hurt in Denver last year, I flew down to stay with her at the hospital where it took the doctors three weeks to fix all the things those men had done to her. She said, *I worry that after something like this I can't believe in God no more.* She said, *Don't let nobody tell you otherwise, this world is a terrible place to be.* Sometimes I feel like all it will take is one more thing—any small thing—and that will be it, I don't know what I'll do. It's the way I felt after Jamie was born, when his birth and Howard's had blurred together so I couldn't tell them apart and each day met the next day in a single, seamless scream.

This morning, arriving home from work at dawn, I found the front porch slick with goose droppings. And there they were, roosting on the lip of the concrete flower box, hissing somewhere deep in their throats. Their eyes opened wider, diamond-hard, shining over my too-tight uniform, the SECURITY badge sewn to my left breast pocket, the empty radio sling bumping my belly, the squeaky black shoes. *You look like a man in that thing,* Foster said the first time he'd seen me in it. But the geese were not fooled—it was me that they saw, and they slithered down from the flower box, stretching their wide white wings like angels, blocking my path. I stared into their gaunt open mouths. Then I went around to Alma's side of the house, let myself in through the old mud room, and crossed through Alma's kitchen to reach the stairs leading up to where Foster and the boys were still sleeping. I set the table, put out cereal and toast and donuts, fixed a cup of hot, black coffee to wash down the ache in my throat. The sun began rising; one bloody knuckle peeked over the horizon and the flooded fields took up the color until the land around the house burned wild fire. And then there were the boys, stumbling into the kitchen with their eyes caked full of sleep. And then there was Foster in his fresh-ironed shirt and sweet cologne, telling them they better hustle up.

At noon, I wake up wet with perspiration, the bed sheets coiled around me and the smell of my polyester uniform caught deep in my hair. I shower and put on my robe, go into the kitchen where I make two grilled Velveeta sandwiches. The boys' old cat, Elephant, twirls between my legs, staring up at me adoringly with his single gooey eye. His stomach and paws are caked with field mud; there is mud beneath Foster's chair at the table, mud on the welcome mat at the top of the stairs, mud on the boys' tennis shoes, impossibly huge, with those wide, lounging tongues. The south edge of the lawn is still under water, and the fields reflect the scarred underbellies of the apple trees, the harsh coin of the sun rippling between them. A few straggly rows of corn grip the high ground, but for the most part the crop is gone, the season's seed lost to the sky. I cut each sandwich into four neat triangles, let a drip of cheese fall to the floor for Elephant. Then I grab a carton of milk, tuck a bag of cookies under my chin, and carry everything down the stairs to Alma.

The sound of Alma's cough, soapy and deep, hangs in the air. Her heart and lungs are slowly filling up with water, and she spends her days at the kitchen table doing crossword puzzles, reading from the Bible, and listening to baseball on the portable radio. She no longer has the energy left to pretend she isn't dying. Foster and I have rented the upstairs ever since Howard was born, and when Alma passes on I don't know what we'll do. But Foster doesn't seem to be worried. "An old woman like that," he says, "goes on for years and years." Last night after supper, while I got ready for work, he and the boys rode their dirt bikes up and down the long muddy driveway to the road even though Alma has asked them not to do this. Alma has also asked them not to lean their bikes against her altar to the Virgin beneath the chestnut tree; she has asked them not to walk through what's left of her perennial bed; she has begged them to pen up the geese which are eating her lawn and have taken to roosting in the shed. Mornings, they spread out beneath the old swing set, quarreling in their school-girl voices and tearing up tufts of drowned grass. I hate the smooth snake weave of their necks, the pale slabs of their tongues. I hate the way they lower their heavy white bodies into the watery hollows beneath the swings, overly careful of themselves, like rich people putting on airs.

Alma is sleeping in a straight-backed chair, her head dangling loose from her shoulders exposing the round pink cap of her skull. Her kitchen is just like mine, except that the walls are papered in blue, and last year she had new wood cupboards and a formica countertop installed to celebrate her seventy-fifth birthday. The old countertop was made of slate, and when the boys were small Alma would lift them up there so we could trace their bodies in chalk. Then we'd help them to draw in their features—bulging muscles, mustaches and beards, bushy eyebrows—things that came to mind when we imagined them as men.

She wakes up when I set her sandwich in front of her. "Time to eat already?" Her voice is rusty, Elephant's tired mew.

"It is."

"You didn't have to go through the trouble."

"Easy to cook for two as one."

We pretend that these are not the same things we say to each other every day. When we bow our heads for Grace, there's a commotion on the front porch, and I open my eyes to see the diamond eye of a goose gleaming through the window. "Amen," Alma says, and she turns to look too. "Do you believe that?" she says. "Up on the back of the porch chair! Fixing to come in and grab our lunch, I would guess."

She pries open one of her sandwich triangles to scoop out a bit of cheese.

"It's the kind you like," I tell her.

"I like everything," Alma says, and she licks the cheese from her finger, but she puts down her sandwich without eating any more of it. It's hard for her to swallow; lately, even the act of chewing wears her out. But she drinks her milk in thick swallows, and when she finishes she says, "So how is Sarah Beth?"

Alma is the only person who still asks after my sister. With Foster, just like with my friends from our church, it's as if she has simply disappeared. In all the old stories about the saints, women died *protecting their virtue.* Saint Maria Goretti. Saint Cecelia. But my sister survived, and no one knows what to do. "She's taking a jewelry-making class," I say. "She's making me a pair of turquoise earrings."

"Turquoise," Alma says, her voice soft as the blue of the stone itself.

"She could make you something, too," I say eagerly, but Alma shakes her head.

"There's nothing like that I need. Though I wish there was." I can see the delicate flutter of the pulse at her neck. "I wish I could think of something."

Another goose has clambered up onto the back of the porch chair. It beats its powerful wings, thumping the side of the house. "You got to admire them," Alma says, twisting to see. "Once they get an idea in their heads, it don't shake loose."

"I'm still after the boys about that fence," I say, hating the high, defensive note in my voice. "Foster says they'll get to it."

"After I'm dead and gone, I suppose," Alma says mildly, and it hurts because it's probably true. More geese appear in the window, popping up like a bright-eyed garden of weeds, long necks swaying. The look of them makes me shiver. Last week they chased me all the way to the truck as Foster and the boys watched from the window, laughing.

"I get on them about that fence every day," I say, and with that the geese tip the porch chair with a terrible crash. "*Ach*," Alma cries, "I bet they broke that old thing!" She gets up, coughing, and moves to the window to see, clinging to the edge of the table for balance. I get up too, but then I sit down because the only thing I can think of to do is to go out there and shoo them off. I imagine how they'll fling their round white bodies at me, beating me down to the porch floor. I smell their hot, goose breath, feel the points of their beaks digging into me.

"Come look," Alma says. I can't believe she is laughing. "So many feathers! It's like a pillow fight."

I say, "I'm sure I'll see enough of them the next time they chase me around the house."

"They bother you that bad?" Alma says. "You just got to show 'em who's the boss."

"I guess I'm not meant to be anybody's boss," I say. "It's not in my personality," and I begin eating cookies, stuffing them down one after another, hoping I won't cry. Alma starts to cough, but checks it. Her face darkens for a moment. "You come with me," she says, low in her throat so I know she is serious, and I follow her slow walk out of the kitchen, through the mud room, and onto the porch. The geese flutter and hiss, but Alma has been seized with a strange, bright energy. "I know you don't like to hear it, but you got to stick up for yourself, Marilee!"

"I *do*," I say, knowing it's a lie. The geese roll at us like a terrible wave and I step back in spite of myself. Alma grabs the broom from its hook beneath the awning. "Watch!" she says. She swings the broom into the side of the closest, plumpest goose. "G'wan!" she grunts, and all the geese tumble off the porch, skittering through the puddles until they reach the edge of the fields. "Promise me," Alma says. "Promise you'll remember this." Then she begins to cough. Her mouth hangs open, purple-lipped, and I catch her as she goes down on her knees. The cough shakes her body, long twisting spasms that remind me of birth pains, how they get worse just when it seems they simply can't.

I help her back into the house, put her into a clean nightgown. "So tired," Alma says as I guide her into bed. I bring the radio in from the kitchen, but she says to shut it off, and my stomach falls into a hot, queasy pit that I imagine must be hell. I'm thirty-two years old, healthy and strong; it would have been nothing for me to run off those geese, but I couldn't do it, even for Alma. It strikes me that she could die right now, and for the first time I imagine how it will be to live somewhere else with Foster and the boys and miles of land all around us, and every night driving to work, and every day coming home, and my sister writing letter after letter saying, *I don't know that I can believe in anything now.* And the shame that I feel is worse than what I felt the last time I called in a false alarm, the time that I saw—*I saw*—someone outside the building with his pants down, his parts pressed against the glass. For weeks, Max Bolton wouldn't leave it alone. What you got to worry about? he'd say. A man would pop one of these pretty mannequins before he'd take one look at you. It was

Foster who heard from a friend in town that it had been Max all along.

I cannot bear the thought of going back upstairs, so I get into bed beside Alma, draw the covers up to my chin. Her body next to mine is like a child's, but the smell of her is different, sharper, strange. It's one o'clock, and if I sleep till five, I'll have had the eight hours I am told are all that anyone actually needs. I awaken at four thirty to the sound of the geese beneath the bedroom window, fighting each other with their bright beaks, their blustery wings. And, still, I do not go back upstairs.

I get to work late, pulling into the flooded parking lot so fast that the water splashes up over my windshield. The department store is deathly hot; the air-conditioning system is down, and without the big blowing sound coming from the vents, the building seems smaller. As I pass the mannequin children in their stiff new clothes, I notice the dust that has settled along the rims of their ears, the full, rosy bottoms of their lips. I lick my finger and try to rub them clean, but instead I leave a series of smudges, each one like a delicate bruise. The children's expressions are accusing now. I pull up the little girl's knee socks apologetically, rolling the tops the way I wore them at her age, confident in my own bright saddle shoes and already flirting with shy country boys like Foster. But I can see that she doesn't forgive me; her bruised smile is a sneer. I leave her that way, heading back to the windowless office where I drop off my magazines, my stationery, my purse.

The office always smells of Max Bolton: cigars, fried meat, English Leather cologne. There's a desk which we are supposed to share, a chair, a hot plate for instant coffee, and a TV screen that broadcasts three scenes: the front entrances, the fire door, and the central isle that runs the length of the building like a backbone. The mannequin bride hovers at the far end, a frail white blossom, a ghost. I glance at the screens, but things look the way they do every night, fuzzy and grayed, like people in an old photograph. A second bride watches me from a single brass frame on the desk; she is Max Bolton's daughter, Elizabeth, married June 18, 1987. I know because I have slipped the photo from behind its glass guard to read the back. I go through the pockets of the jackets he leaves on the hook behind the door. I jimmy the desk drawers with paper clips, rustle through shopping lists, sci-fi novels, half-written letters, unpaid bills.

You leave everything the way you found it, he told me when I first started work in January, and from the way that he said it, I knew he'd set traps, that he would be watching to make sure I obeyed. Foster had just started school, and I'd been lucky to get this job: no experience, a quick GED, my only reference written by Max as a favor to Foster. So I did not touch the centerfold of Miss July which was taped to the seat of the chair, her mouth open wide, her eyes pleading. I did not move the breast-shaped coffee mug with its pointed red nipple. But I began to look for small secret clues I could chant like a spell when I ran into Max on the street, at The Fisco where Foster likes to drink, at the main office picking up our paychecks. *His daughter won't come home to visit. His truck got repossessed.*

I sign in, pick up my radio, and begin the first of my rounds. The department store used to belong to International Harvester, and to-night I notice the bitter odor of diesel underneath the new-carpet smell of polyester and dye. I remember the gleaming combines and balers standing in rows like animals as my sister and I walked between them, holding my grandfather's hands. How badly we wanted to climb up on the tractors! but he worried that we might fall, and he kept a cautious eye on us while he talked his business with the jolly sales rep, a skinny bald man who gave us each a sucker for being so quiet, so good. That same night my grandfather died of a massive coronary, and when the harvester he'd signed for arrived a week later, no one knew what to do. Sometimes, I wonder how often I've passed over the very spot where the three of us stood, my sister and I working our tongues around our suckers until we'd melted those hard, sweet stones. At the funeral, we were lifted up to kiss my grandfather's silent cheek, but we were not afraid. We knew it was the spirit of a person—not that person's body—which mattered, which was real.

In the hot, still air I hear the whisper of fabric brushing fabric—or is it just the sound of my own breathing? Perhaps it's my grandfather's ghost, watching me pass through Household Appliances into Lingerie. I imagine him rustling between the half-slips and bras, cracking the stumps of his broken-off fingers like he always did to make me smile. Alma's husband has appeared to her twice: once on the first anniversary of his death, once when she was tempted to remarry. My sister has seen the men who attacked her standing at the foot of her bed, in broad daylight, plain as if they were real.

"You're not being rational," Foster said, after I told him I planned to live downstairs with Alma till he and the boys got that fence put up like they'd promised. I'd already packed an overnight bag; I had my uniform, my purse, my keys. "Marilee," he pleaded, "it's suppertime." I thanked him for the reminder, and then I cooked me and Alma Swedish meatballs and green beans and fresh corn muffins. I served her in bed like she was a queen, and together we pretended that she wasn't sick, that I wasn't afraid to go back into the kitchen in case Foster came down the stairs. We could tell by the thumps and the scraping of chairs that he was starting to get angry; several times, I heard him yelling at the boys. After supper, I shot out of the house so fast that the geese blew in all directions like pieces of a thick meringue pie. By the time I'd locked myself in the truck, I could see Foster in the doorway, but I looked the other way and drove off slow, as if I couldn't care less. Foster, with his easy walk, his shoulders slumped just so. Foster with his hands in my hair, his mouth over mine, speaking my name. Foster, when I wake up dreaming of my sister, saying, *Honey, I'd never let that happen to you.*

My heavy black shoes go *screek, screek,* but beneath that sound I still hear the swish of fabric—a man's trouser legs swiping against each other? I reach for my radio, but then I remember the disgust of the officer the last time he showed up to find only me and the empty night air. I force myself to walk extra-slow through Sports and Recreation, past the racks of hunting rifles, the display case filled with clever hand guns, neat as a row of hairdryers. *Don't look back!* I hear my sister say, and I plan to keep right on walking until I'm safe in the windowless office, but then I hear the soft click, click of a man's light tiptoe. This is no ghost. This is no game. There is someone else in the building, and my stomach gets small and hard and tight as I think about Max's pale body pressed against the window. Again I smell that acrid odor of diesel, stronger, too strong, I realize, to be leftover from the past.

As I step out into the center aisle, the bride abruptly comes to life, the skirt of her white white gown rippling hard as if she is walking toward me. Her arms embrace the open air; her fingers are sharp, naked bones. She is smiling like something out of a fairy tale, the good witch turned evil. As her skirt lifts again, I see the oscillating fan tucked underneath, its neck clicking like a tired joint, and there's the cord poking out from under the lacy layers. I walk around behind the bride's platform and kick the plug out of the wall socket. The fan's motor grunts one last time and quits, but it's hot, still heating, melting the rubber coating off the wires. *Max,* I think. *He must have thought to scare me.* And with that thought, the bride's dress catches fire.

In a single startling moment of clarity, I understand that if the fire alarm goes off, I will not be able to explain this. I knock the bride from her pedestal, grab her by the long flow of her hair and drag her, bouncing madly behind me, toward the wide double doors at front entrance. My keys are a wild jangle at my hips; I fumble the right one into the lock and kick the bride into the entryway. She's smoking badly now, a harsh chemical smoke, and I hold my breath as I unlock the last door. Her head pops off, rolling end over end, so I pick her up by her slender neck and throw her, feet first, into the flooded parking lot. She lands in a thick hiss of steam. I turn her with my foot until she's wet on all sides, I kick her, I kick her again, and by the time the last of the smoke clears away, I have decided what I want to do next. I find her head just inside the door and carry it back to the security office, where I stuff it into one of Max's desk drawers.

But it's not enough. My anger has taken hold, its own sudden fire, gloriously out of control. In Denver, half conscious, my sister used words worse than anything the boys would ever say, words I'd seen only in the sort of magazines that Foster keeps hidden at the back of our bedroom closet. She was one long broken bone, but when I touched her cheek, she bit my hand and then kept on cursing, cursing as I cried. Later on, when the priest on call talked about forgiveness, Sara Beth closed her eyes. *Anger will eat you up inside,* the priest had said. But now I understand how it burns us clean.

I go back out to the parking lot and get what's left of the bride's body; I wrestle her inside and down the isle and into the security office where I arrange her, scorched and dripping, in Max's chair. I wedge his nipple mug into the melted grasp of her fingers. And then I write FUCK YOU MAX on an envelope and pin it to what's left of her chest.

Suddenly I feel calm and good, the way I do after Mass when I almost believe that things will work out right, no matter how bad they seem. The building still smells of diesel, so I prop the front doors open wide and leave them that way until the last trace of smoke is gone for good. I mop up the messy trail left by the bride's wet gown, carry her white platform into storage, rearrange the racks of clothing and put the burned-out fan in the dumpster out back. By dawn, everything looks the way it usually does, orderly and cluttered all at once. I lock up slowly, carefully, knowing it will be the last time I ever do so. I'll get another job, I tell myself, a better one. Something during the day so I can spend time with the boys—*my* boys. Maybe I'll go back to school myself, become a physician's assistant or even a nurse, someone who knows how to help other people like those counselors in Denver helped my sister.

I drive home into the sun's rising eye with my windows rolled down, the wind singing in my hair. The flood waters stretch for miles, lapping and licking, the bright, wet sound of want. When I turn down the driveway leading to the house, the truck bounces over the potholes, shaking me like a mother's scolding hand, but I hang on. It's true dawn now, the dark limbs of the trees scorching the cherry sky. The silo hums with pigeons. Mourning doves coo on the clothesline. There, on the high ground beside the house, stands the new chicken-wire fence and, within it, the sleepy flutter of geese. Balloons of every color flare from the stakes, knocking their heads in the wind. And upstairs, the light in our bedroom is shining, faint as the first morning star.